Lost Temptation

Angelina Ross

ISBN: 1450543081
ISBN-13: 9781450543088
Library of Congress Control Number: 2010900975

This book is dedicated to my grandmother, Constance,
who helped to make my dreams come true.

PROLOGUE

She hurried along the beach looking over her shoulder to be certain she was not followed. The moonlight was shining brightly, exposing her for anyone to see. When she was sure she was alone she continued on to her destination, pulling her hood farther over her head and willing her feet to move faster. Minutes later she spotted what she was looking for. A lone girl waited pacing back and forth in the surf on the beach, her long flaxen hair blowing in the wind. She looked up, spotting the cloaked figure moving toward her.

"Asta!" The girl sighed, reaching out to hug her friend.

"Phaedra, did you think I would not make it? I had to be sure I was not followed before I could slip out of the village." Asta hugged her friend back and looked out toward the water. "Where is the ship?"

"It's out there," Phaedra said, pointing toward the darkness. "Look out below the bright star. She sits below it."

"Yes. I see it."

The ship was black, dark as night itself. Even with the clear skies and bright moon, it was only noticeable if you were looking for it. Its massive frame was bobbing in the water as if waiting to be let loose.

Asta looked at the distance between the ship and the beach where they stood. This would be it. Once they left there would be no turning back. Asta looked to her friend.

"Are you sure you want to do this?"

"I am not going to drown if that's what you mean."

"It's not. Are you sure you want to come with me, Phaedra? It could be dangerous, more dangerous than anything we have been through before."

The trip across the North Sea would take some time, but when they reached their destination they needed to be strong. While the lands around Vestfold could be dangerous, they were still familiar. This new land they were travelling to was not for it had been many years since Asta had put her eyes on its high mountains and mystical lochs.

"Asta, we are the best of friends, sisters, if I may say. Wherever you go, I will be by your side, no matter what the dangers."

Asta let out a breath she didn't even realize she was holding. "Then we must go now, before we are found out." She removed her cloak and stuffed it into her bag. Then she tied her waist with a leather strip, and the other end she tied around Phaedra.

Together they walked into the water, slipping through the waves and making their way to the ship. At the edge of the ship they grasped the ladders that had been let down for them. Phaedra climbed over the side to the deck, untying herself. Asta swung her bag over the edge of the ship and climbed aboard before noticing a dozen bodies huddled around the deck.

"What is this?" Asta hissed, clenching her fists to her sides.

"Calm yourself, Asta. Do you want to frighten them?" The figure walked from the shadows into the moon's path, her long, raven hair catching the light and turning it almost blue.

"What have you done, Freya?" Asta looked around, realizing these were all young women. "Oh no, please tell me you didn't do it." Asta searched her friend's face hoping she had made a mistake.

"I couldn't leave them there. They would be destroyed. You know what that's like, Asta. You've seen it, even lived it."

"We can't take the risk of getting caught."

"If we take them back we will risk getting caught. Torum will punish us all."

Asta knew exactly what he would do. She reached up absently, rubbing her shoulders. He would be angry when he found they were gone. But not as angry as when he found she was gone too. She shivered at the image that flashed through her mind from that thought. She took a deep breath and exhaled. "Can they work the ship?"

At these words the entire ship came to life. Freya moved across the ship barking orders as Phaedra followed, helping each girl to their task. As the vessel began to glide across the open water, Asta turned to take one last look at the land she had called home for so many years. A small fear gripped her, but she quickly pushed it to the back of her mind.

"Saying good-bye to your old life?" Phaedra gently laid her hand on Asta's shoulder.

"You could say that." Asta watched as the land faded into the distance. This was the beginning of a new life—and a new adventure.

The lightning streaked across the sky, outlining the form that was crouched down beside the boulder. Knees bent, arms ready, Jorund pulled back on his bow, keeping his eye on his target. The storm above gave him light as the thunder roared through the trees. There was a movement in the distance, but it was too late. He let his arrow loose, missing its mark, and he stood watching as the great deer ran off into the forest. Cursing loudly, he looked back to where it had stood. His mind was playing tricks on him, for in that split second as the lightning lit the sky, he had seen a girl walking through the forest. He moved toward the area he had seen her in. The morning gray was creeping in, but the storm was keeping his surroundings dark. He spotted his arrow in the distant bushes and went to retrieve it. But as he reached for it he froze. The lightning once again illuminated the sky, exposing the woman's still form. She was lying on the ground, her long, dark hair spread out around her, his arrow protruding from her side.

Jorund dropped to his knees, ripping open her shirt to get a better look at the wound. The arrow was in her side and he could clearly see the dark spot spreading across her pale skin. He removed his cloak, tearing it into several pieces and setting them aside. He lifted her to see how far the arrow had gone in.

It was through all the way so he broke off the tip and pulled the remaining piece through. The girl opened her eyes and a low moan escaped from her lips. Her blue eyes stared at him for seconds before closing again.

He pressed a piece of the torn cloth onto her back to help stop the bleeding then did the same to the front. He wrapped the remaining cloth around her to hold the padding. Once done he picked her up and walked back to the clearing where he had left his horse. He carefully mounted with her in his arms and rode back to his village.

He rode through the village gates just as the rain started to fall again. It was still early and many were just rising, but he kept on toward the tower, ignoring their startled and curious faces. Once at the gates he demanded the guards to open them and waited impatiently as they rushed to do his bidding. His hand was moist on her back and he knew the wound was still bleeding. He growled loudly, kicking his horse into a gallop, and entered through the moving gates before they were completely open, scaring the boy who was loading a wagon. Jorund stopped and dismounted his horse all in one swift move, cautious not to cause anymore harm to his precious cargo.

"Ian! Take my horse to the stables, then fetch Gunnar," Jorund yelled over his shoulder as he made his way into the tower.

The boy jumped from the wagon and did as he was told.

Jorund entered the great hall, making his way toward the stairs. The fire pit was ablaze so he knew Dania had risen. She emerged from the kitchen, her short, plump frame dirty from cooking, her copper hair coiled high on her head, small wisps escaping the sides.

"What is—" There was a sharp intake of breath before she continued, "Jorund, what have you done? Who is she? Why is she—"

"I need hot water and towels. The doc is on his way. When he gets here, send him to my room." He climbed to the top of the stairs, turning right, and made his way down the walk to the last door. He pushed it open and headed for the bed, gently laying her on the furs.

Dania entered with the hot water and towels, putting them next to the bed. Together they unwound the makeshift bandages and undressed her, leaving only a blanket for cover. Dania retrieved one of Jorund's shirts and put it on the bed for later.

"One more thing, I need you to help me hold her. The doc will take too long and I need to stop the bleeding. We need to sear the wound closed."

Dania nodded her response and left to get the hot pan and an iron rod.

Jorund took a clean cloth and put it into the water, then he took the dry ones and layered them on the bed, moving her gently to lay them beneath her. Reaching in the water he took the wet cloth, lifting the blanket to clean the wounds then inspected the first where the arrow had entered and the second where it tried to exit. The bleeding had slowed, but the wounds were open and deep.

As he waited for Dania's return, he took a moment to look over the girl. Her long, auburn hair was spread out across the pillow, curling up at the ends. Her cheek bones were high, her face smooth, with a tint of color from the sun giving her skin a slight glow. She was beautiful, every man's dream of a gorgeous woman. But she wasn't dressed like any women he knew. She wore trousers, a wool shirt, and a cape, as if she was trying to hide the fact that she was, indeed, a woman. No woman around here would be in the woods alone, which brought the question, where was she from? And as he rode with her he had relieved her of seven daggers stashed among various parts of her body.

Dania entered the room and set the hot coals next to the bed. Jorund took the iron rod from her and set it in the hot coals. Then turning his attention to the girl, he cleaned the wound one more time before beginning.

It was much later when the door opened and the doc walked in, his hair tousled and breathing heavily.

"I almost thought you were not coming, Gunnar." Jorund finished piling the stained towels next to the door.

"What happened?" Gunnar's gaze went from the pile of blood-soaked towels to the still form on the bed. "Is she alive?"

"Yes, she is alive. It was an accident." Jorund followed him to the bed. "I was out hunting in the forest and missed the deer."

"And hit her instead?" Gunnar peeked through the slit Jorund had made in the shirt she now wore. "Was there much bleeding?"

"Yes, at first. But it slowed after a while. I wrapped it tight before I brought her here." They both stood there staring at her until Gunnar broke the long silence.

"What do you think she was doing out there?"

"I don't know, but I found these on her." Jorund went to the table for his bag. Reaching inside he pulled out the daggers and spread them across the table.

Gunnar ran his fingertips across the ivory handles of the knives, picking one up to better examine it. "Why would she need so many?" he asked, putting it back with the others.

"I don't know, and I won't know until she wakes up and tells us." Jorund placed the daggers back in the bag and handed it to Gunnar. "I think you should keep these until I find out." Jorund glanced back at the bed, curious about the strange girl.

He didn't tell Gunnar about the deep scars on her back that he and Dania had seen while changing her. That was something they would keep to themselves.

"She will rest for now. I'm going for food. Are you joining me?"

"Have I ever turned down food?" Gunnar answered, laughing and rubbing his stomach.

"Good. I need someone with me when I tell Dania what happened."

Gunnar's laughter continued as they left the room.

Who was he? She could hear his voice soothing her, taking away the nightmares. Why was he here? She felt a cool cloth being placed on her forehead. She tried to push it away, but there was a strong force holding her down.

"You need to relax. Everything is going to be fine. You're safe."

She felt the warmth of his breath as he spoke to her. He smelled of fresh cut wood and salty sea. She tried to open her eyes but the blackness took over, keeping her prisoner.

The sun was setting slowly, casting the room into shadows.

"It's been four days. Do you think she will recover?" Jorund was pacing back and forth across Dania's room as she sat in her chair by the window.

"She is no longer thrashing about with fever, so I would say her chances are good. I know you are impatient to get your answers, but give her a few more days. She has been through a lot." Dania placed her cloth and stitching needle back into its basket and walked to Jorund, placing her hand on his arm so he had no choice but to stop pacing. "What good will you be to anyone if you have no rest?" She escorted him out of her room and up the walk to his brother's room where he had been staying.

"Now try to sleep, son, and I will stay with her tonight." She stood there waiting for an objection, but Jorund looked too weary to argue. He entered the room and closed the door behind him.

Dania made her way to the room where the young girl slept. A cot had been placed at the end of the bed for Jorund to sleep on, but it had not been touched. Instead he had pulled the chair from the window, putting it next to the bed, and had perched himself there since his arrival back to the tower with her. He had not left her side with the exception of the few times he was needed to check the progress of the festival they were preparing for. He had even taken his meals here, though she could see by the full platter of food on the table that he wasn't even eating. Never had she seen her son attend to a female so intently. For Jorund's sake she hoped this girl would wake up soon.

Dania sat in the chair, head back, watching the girl as she slept. Something familiar tugged at the back of her mind. But she shrugged it off and closed her eyes.

The most intoxicating scent drifted up to Asta's nose, shattering her dreams and bringing her out of her deep slumber. She inhaled deeper, recognizing the smell of the ocean mingled with a light floral scent. She rubbed her hand across the smooth surface of the bed she was lying in. She slowly opened her eyes, trying hard to see through the haze. Where was she?

Her eyes finally focused and she examined her surroundings. She looked to the door, but it was closed to the world beyond. Next to her was a dark wood wardrobe, its huge doors carved deep with a trail of vines outlining each door, the handles shaped leaves dipped in gold. The same design adorned the four wooden posts of the great bed she was lying in. On the top of each post was a golden leaf, its stem curved into a hook to hold the layers of black-blue silk that cascaded down each corner. The bed itself was covered in furs and silks of various colors while many pillows lined the bed behind her. She turned her head to the other side and there stood a large iron candelabra, its candles burnt down, leaving a mass of wax upon the floor.

The window was next; the shutters open wide, letting the cool breeze in. Below it stood a small wooden table on which a jar of flowers sat. Sitting with the table was a large, menacing chair, its wood stained to match the other furniture. A few red pillows had been thrown on it for comfort. The arms and legs were carved with dragon heads; their mouths open wide showing a great row of teeth.

She tried to sit up to see the rest of the room, but it started to spin so she lay her head back down on the pillow and thought back to the last thing she could remember.

It had been four day's since Freya and the other girls had left Asta and Phaedra off the coast before continuing on their journey to Ireland. Most of the girls, including Freya, had been abducted from the lush land and those who had never been there went with new hopes.

After three days of walking the land, Asta and Phaedra finally settled into the forest for a much needed rest. Asta had awakened early to search for the stones, leaving Phaedra to sleep until sunrise. She moved quickly through the forest hoping to return to Phaedra before the rain started to fall. She had been walking a while when a deer crossed her path. It stood there for a moment looking at her before it turned and moved in the opposite direction. Then everything went so fast. The lightning lit the sky, the deer ran, and pain consumed her body.

Asta took deep breaths to relax, but panic was rising in her. She sat up and swung her legs over the edge of the bed. The pain hit her like the blow of a large fist. She sat motionless, teeth clenched, trying to get control of her body. Someone had changed her into a large wool shirt that had been split on the side, exposing a large bandage wrapped around her middle. She opened the split wider and pulled the bandage down.

She stared in shock at the two neatly burned rows. One was at the front of her lower stomach, the other at the back of her side. There was no bleeding and they were seared closed, but the skin was swollen and red. She pulled the bandage back down over the wound. The room started to spin and her stomach started to churn. She very slowly started to lie back down, grunting from the pain with each movement.

"Please, let me help you."

Asta looked up to see a short, plump woman carry a tray across the room to the table by the window. Her hair was tightly coiled atop her head, but that didn't stop the sun from bringing out its true copper color.

The woman set the tray down and turned to the bed to help Asta. "My name is Dania..."

Her step faltered and her smile faded, but only for a moment before she was next to the bed moving pillows and helping Asta get comfortable. Then she went to the table and picked up a mug, returning to the bed.

"Where am I?" Asta asked through clenched teeth. The pain was intensifying at a rapid degree.

"This will help to ease the pain." Dania put the mug into Asta's hands then returned to the tray and came back with a damp cloth, placing it on Asta's forehead.

Asta sipped on the spicy concoction, trying not to spill it. The pain was so bad now that she didn't care if it was poison. She would gladly take death over this torture.

"You are safe here. I know you have many questions, but let's work on getting you better first." Dania took the mug from Asta's relaxing body.

"I need to go. I can't stay." Asta wanted to leave, but the blackness started to take her. Images of a young girl floated through her mind.

"You still have a slight fever. Just rest and in a few days you will be feeling much better."

"What about Phaedra?" Asta whispered as her mind slipped into the dark abyss.

The night was cold, the small cave colder. Phaedra curled up and wrapped herself in both cloaks. How she longed for a fire, but there had been voices in the night. She was sure she did not want to get caught in a cave by so many men, even though the ivy hung down, hiding the entrance from anyone who would walk by. She had provisions for a few more days, but if Asta did not come back, she would have to head toward the coast. She would decide what to do from there.

Why would Asta leave and not tell her where she was going? In all their years together they had never been apart. Something had to have happened for her to be gone for so long. Tomorrow she would leave a sign. Hopefully Asta would come for her.

Jorund entered the tower after a long and weary day. Some of the men needed help setting up for the festival and his mother had kindly volunteered him.

"It will do you some good to get outside."

"I do get outside."

"Only for quick minutes before you're rushing back here to see if she is awake. If she does wake I will send someone to get you."

Now he headed for the stairs and his bed that was quietly beckoning to him. After helping the men, they had insisted he go sit with them and drink. Time had slipped by and it was now late into the night. As he reached the top floor, he noticed light spilling from under Dania's door. He knocked lightly, waiting for a response.

"Come in."

Jorund opened the door, but instead of being in bed, Dania was fully dressed sitting in the chair by the window.

"Mother, why are you still awake?" Jorund asked, stepping into the room.

Dania set the mug she was holding onto the table next to her and turned toward Jorund. "I was thinking of that woman in the other room. Are you sure she was alone? It seems very unusual that she was in the forest by herself.

"If someone had been with her, I would know. They would not have let me take her and I may just be dead," he stated flatly, hoping she would change the subject.

The same thought had crossed his mind time and again. Why would a beautiful young woman be wandering through the forest alone? And there were the scars. She had so many. Someone had hurt her. During her frenzied nights of feverish sleep it was Jorund who took the brute force of her fists as she fought the attacker in her dreams.

Torum.

That is the name she had cried out as she fought to be free. And it was Jorund's soft whispers of reassurance that calmed her enough to rest. But Dania was right. Questions he wanted answers to would have to wait.

"You go to sleep and I will check on her," he said, turning to leave.

"I spoke to her today," Dania said, turning back to the window.

Jorund stopped halfway out the door and turned back around. "What did she say? And why didn't you come for me?" he asked, eager to know what had happened.

"I was taking her some tonic, for I heard her from my room groaning."

"Groaning from the pain?"

"She was trying to get out of bed. I helped her back and told her my name."

"Did she say anything?"

"She asked where she was."

"And what did you tell her?" Jorund was leaned against the door frame arms crossed, all attention on Dania.

She turned in the chair once again to face Jorund. "I told her it would be best if she was better before she worried about anything else. I also told her she was safe and to rest. She fell asleep whispering."

"Whispering what?" he asked curiously.

"She said 'what about Phaedra?'"

"Phaedra? Who is Phaedra? My men searched the forest for two days looking for signs of anyone or anything that would tell us who she was." He said nodding in the direction of the sleeping form. "They came back with nothing." Jorund thought back to the first time she had appeared. She was like a spirit coming through the forest, rising from the mist. But spirits can't be touched. They can't be held in your arms as he had held her.

"Jorund! Are you listening to me?" Dania rose from her chair and walked to her son. "I asked if you think Phaedra may be family."

"Until she wakes and gives us answers we will not know." He kissed her on the cheek. "Go to sleep, it is late." He closed the door behind him and headed down the walkway toward his room. That is where he had taken her six days ago when he brought her here. His room. His bed.

The first few days she was here had been the worst. By day three her fever had reached its highest. She had awakened kicking and screaming. It took Dania and himself to hold her down and pour the tonic into her mouth. By the time they had calmed her, she had managed to reopen the wounds. But with the strength of the potion, he was able to sear them closed without her even moving.

He reached the door and slowly opened it to peek inside. He could see the outline of her body in the bed, the blanket rising and falling with each breath she took. Her fever had broken the past night and she had slept quietly since. He closed the door and headed to his brother's room. How nice it would be to have a good night's sleep.

The light was appearing small at first then becoming brighter. Was she dead? She couldn't be, for the pain in her head was very real. Asta opened her eyes to the rising sun's glow coming in from the open window.

There stood Dania.

She was arranging fresh-cut flowers on the table. The breeze carried the scent to Asta's nose and she inhaled deeply. Dania heard and turned to look at her.

"So, you're awake. I was hoping it would be soon." She left the room but returned minutes later bearing a tray with food and drink. She placed the tray on the table and picked up the mug, carrying it to the bed.

"Drink this. It will help with the pain." Dania handed the mug to Asta.

"No, I don't want to sleep anymore." Asta raised her hand and pushed the mug away.

Dania only smiled and explained to Asta that it was not the same. "It will help ease the pain, but you will not sleep."

Asta sat up in the bed with the help of Dania then took the mug, sipping it slowly. Within a few moments the pain in her head and side started to subside.

"How long have I been here?" Asta asked, giving the empty mug back to Dania.

"Eight days. We weren't sure if you were going to make it at first. You have a strong will to live." Dania said, returning the mug to the tray.

"Who is the other person?"

"What?"

"You said 'we weren't sure'."

Dania went to the bed and sat with Asta. "How much do you remember about coming here?"

Asta hesitated a moment before answering. "Nothing at all. I was walking through the forest when I came upon this huge deer. It turned and ran then everything went black."

"My son was hunting that deer. You came into his path and he shot you."

"He shot me?"

"It was an accident. Jorund is good with a bow and arrow and would never have been so careless. But he didn't expect you to materialize from the forest."

Asta watched Dania's posture become straighter as she defended her son.

"I would not doubt your word that your son, Jorund, made an honest mistake. As he was not expecting me, I also was not expecting him." Asta leaned back against the pillows. "If it was otherwise, I am sure I would not have had the great care that I have received here."

"I thank you for the compliment, but it is my son who deserves the praise," Dania said, smiling big and patting Asta's hand.

She stood and went to the tray. "He brought you here and mended your wounds. And it was he who stayed by your side as you battled for days with fever."

So that's the voice she had heard talking her out of her nightmares. It's too bad she would not be around to give her thanks to him. She pulled back the covers and slowly sat on the edge of the bed, ignoring Dania's gasp of surprise. "I will need some clothes. Trousers and a cloak will do," she said, stretching her arms so she could estimate the pain.

"Wouldn't you be more comfortable in a chemise and tunic? It wouldn't be so tight upon your wound."

"It wouldn't be practical for the journey."

"The journey?" The warmth in Dania's eyes turned to panic.

"Of course, I can't stay here forever." Asta watched Dania slowly walk toward the door then pause.

"You're welcome here as long as you want," Dania said, turning back toward Asta. "At least stay until you have had time to heal more."

Asta took a deep breath, cringing at the sharp pain in her side. She knew she should rest more, but the thought of Phaedra, alone in the woods, was enough to make her ignore the pain. "I thank you again for your hospitality. But as we both know, this visit was unplanned, and I do have things I need to return to." Asta gave what she hoped was her best smile.

Dania smiled back and continued toward the door.

"Well, if you change your mind, the offer will still be open," she said, and then she was gone.

Asta practiced walking back and forth from the bed to the window. She looked at the contents of the food on the tray and listened as her stomach sang a gurgling chorus. It wasn't until now that she realized how hungry she was. She took a piece of cheese and chunk of bread from the tray and ate this as she continued walking circles around the room. The pain was easing due to the liquid Dania had given her, but the throbbing was still great, causing a heavy, uncomfortable feeling throughout her body. She stopped at the table, placing the remaining piece of bread back on the tray.

Asta opened her shirt and folded the bandage down to examine the wound. The marks were still swollen but no longer bright red, rather a pale pink. The skin was healing together fine with the exception of a few raw blisters that were now evident. The skin between the two wounds was now bruising. The blacks, blues, and purples covered her side from the bottom of her rib cage to the top of her thigh. She moved her fingers lightly across the bruising and around each wound. It would all eventually heal and movement wouldn't be so difficult. She pulled the bandage back up and closed the gap in her shirt.

A stiff breeze blew through the window, surrounding Asta with the scents of salty sea and the exotic essence from the flowers on the table. Suddenly Asta's mind burst open, flooding with long-forgotten memories. A young girl perched on her mother's lap holding the few flowers she had picked from outside. They sat at an open window letting the cool breeze wash over them as they listened to the ocean crashing below.

Asta braced her hands on the table. Closing her eyes, she took a few deep breaths, trying to push the memories back where they belonged, but to no avail. The sound of the waves crashing below echoed in every corner of the room. She stood straight and opened her eyes, blinking rapidly as tears threatened to spill.

"Are you alright, child?"

Asta hadn't heard Dania enter the room, but she was there with a worried look on her face.

"Is the pain too much? It may be better if you rest some more."

Asta took the clothes from Dania and began to dress. "I have been here too long already."

"Jorund will not be happy I let you leave. He feels that you are his responsibility since he is at fault for your being here."

"I am my own responsibility and I don't need anyone watching over me." Asta knew she sounded harsh, but she didn't want to know these people. It was too dangerous. And since Jorund was the one who brought her here, then he was the one who had taken her weapons. She didn't care if he kept them, they weren't hers anyway. They were just part of a life she wanted to forget, which made one more reason she needed to leave now. He might ask questions she wasn't willing to answer.

Asta paced the room, checking the comfort of the boots while Dania stood to the side of the room watching her with a worried expression.

"They fit perfectly." Asta sat in the chair by the window and, slowly lifting her arms, tried unsuccessfully to tame her long, auburn locks.

"Let me help you." Dania hesitated for a moment, but when Asta made no argument, she swiftly went behind the chair and lightly combed her fingers through Asta's hair. "The clothes are my sons. Well, they were. They are from his youth and no longer fit." Dania smoothed out the last of the knots from Asta's hair and paused for a moment.

"I was wondering…" Dania pulled Asta's hair back and smoothed it into three sections. "Could I ask you a question?" Asta's shoulders rose slightly and tensed. Dania hurried on before Asta had time to react. "You never told me your name and I'm not sure what to call you, but if you don't want to tell me that's fine. It's none of—"

"Asta. My name is Asta."

"Asta." Dania said it out loud, wanting to hear it again. The name did not fit her, but Dania would not tell her that. Not yet anyway. She watched Asta's shoulders relax as she continued to fix her hair. She took each of the sections, twisting them into tight coils atop Asta's head, securing them with pins from her pocket. "There you go. That should keep it up and out of your face for a while."

Asta stood and retrieved the cloak from the bed, dropping it over her arm. "I hope Jorund doesn't mind me taking his clothes."

"They are not Jorund's. They belong to my youngest son, Ranolf. He is away to the Irish coast until the cold returns."

"Well, I'm sure he will not miss them. Now..." Asta opened the door and walked out, "...if you could point me the way I came from, I will be on my way."

It had been hours since Asta had left the sanctuary of the village. The sun still heated a bright path across the sky, peeking its way through the forest roof, but it wouldn't be long before it disappeared, leaving her in the dark. She could not light a fire for the fear of someone seeing her. And though she was good with defense, the only weapon she possessed was the small knife she had taken from the table in the tower's cookery.

At that thought her stomach rolled and protested at its emptiness. She hadn't eaten all day, except the few bites before her departure, and had been walking for hours. Reaching in the bag she carried, she pulled out one of the small melons Dania had insisted she take. Along with that, Dania had packed her bread, cheese, and a few large strips of dried meat. She ate the juicy melon, ignoring the growing pain in her side, and continued through the forest hoping she would soon find a sign from Phaedra.

It was a few minutes later that the first one appeared. Carved into the tree in front of her were three circles perfectly lined with a slash connecting them. She reached up, brushing her fingertips across the rough bark.

Footsteps sounded behind her and she inched her hand down into her bag, holding tightly to the knife.

"Find what you were looking for?"

Asta turned and watched as a man walked through the forest toward her.

"Don't be frightened. My mother sent me."

He stopped a few feet in front of her, his long, muscular legs slightly spread, accentuating his lean waist. His shirt fit tightly across his chest, outlining the ripples in his flat abdomen. His broad shoulders connected to his chiseled arms that were folded across his wide chest.

His wasn't the greatest body she had ever seen, but she would put it up high on her list of gorgeous men.

His raven hair hung straight to his shoulders surrounding an oval face with strong cheekbones. He wore a slight mustache that led into a short beard which made him very attractive.

But it was his eyes that amazed and mesmerized her with their deep pools of brown and sparks of gold. She had a nagging feeling she had seen him before, was sure she had heard his voice. His was the voice that had talked her through her nightmares.

"You're Jorund." It was a statement, not a question, because though she didn't recall ever seeing him, she felt like she already knew him.

"And you are Asta." He stood there staring at her, taking her in from head to toe just as she had done to him.

She cleared her throat to get his attention. "I appreciate your mother's concern, but I will be fine by myself." She turned to leave and heard him follow.

"What are you doing?" she asked, turning back around.

"I'm going with you."

"Why?"

"I'm concerned for you and want to protect you."

"I don't need you to protect me. Good-bye." She walked away, but still he followed her. She stopped and turned around again. "Why are you doing this?"

"I like you and don't want anyone bothering you."

"You don't even know me, and the only person bothering me is you."

A small laugh escaped him. "Someone else might like the chance and I'm not going to let them."

They stood there quietly, eyes locked for what seemed like an eternity. Her side was hurting and she was still very weak. Staying with him wouldn't be such a bad idea. She did need more time to heal. Besides, it would give her a chance to find out how he came to be on this land. Asta broke eye contact and started walking again.

"Are you always this persistent?" she asked, looking over her shoulder.

"Yes," he replied, smiling smugly.

"I'm going to regret this," she said to herself, focusing on the path ahead.

Who was she? Where did she come from? Why did the symbols on the dagger seem familiar to him? There were so many more questions Jorund wanted to ask her, and more arose with each minute he spent around her. Where did she get the scars on her back? Where did the pictures painted on her body come from? What did it mean?

He watched Asta walk away holding her side and followed quietly. Now was not the time to ask. He could see she was still in great amounts of pain and he didn't want to distress her more. He would escort her to find whatever it was she was searching for then he would go home, taking her with him.

He knew she would argue, but he didn't care. He felt a large responsibility for the condition she was in. Though there was something else that drew him to her, he would not admit to it.

Each step she took her body would tense. Gradually she started to put her weight on her good side, causing her to limp. Suddenly she stopped. If he hadn't been watching her so closely, he would have knocked into her.

"The next mark should be here," she said, looking at the trees around her.

"How do you know?" He watched her walk around the small clearing.

"Sixty steps from the first mark. That's how it's done." She continued making her way around the trees.

Jorund walked to the middle of the clearing and slowly spun around scanning the trees. He spotted the sign high above her head. "There it is." He pointed toward the tree and walked out of the clearing, leaving her to follow him.

The third mark was easy to follow, but the path to the fourth was a challenge. When he suggested they rest awhile, she just walked past him, reminding him that he could go home at any time. He followed her up the steep incline, taking the time to study her. Long auburn curls had escaped from her hat and were lying enticingly down her back, ending just below her round derriere. Her legs were long and slender, the pants she wore hiding nothing from his view.

Halfway up, he noticed she was slowing down. He knew she was in pain, but she continued walking, one foot in front of the other. This was enough.

"Stop!" he commanded, continuing toward her.

She stopped and looked at him, her hat slightly tilted to the side, exposing part of her face. She was as pale as a ghost with drops of sweat sliding down her face and pooling at her chin.

"Do you realize you almost died only days ago? You even managed to reopen your wound the first few days you were there." He reached down and scooped her up into his arms, careful not to disrupt her wounds. "You're not completely well and you're out here climbing hills," he said more to himself than to her. "I'm taking you back."

"No," she ground out between clenched teeth. She tried to push her way out of his grip, but she was too weak and her strength was nothing compared to his. Even so, she continued thrashing about in his arms hoping to get free.

He tightened his hold on her to gain her attention. That was a mistake, for his body responded instantly. She finally stopped squirming and looked at him. Her hat had fallen to the ground, leaving her hair free and coming loose from the pins that were holding it. He could now see her eyes clearly for the first time. They were bluer than the clearest ocean water circled by a tint of bright green, her long, dark lashes surrounding them to give her an almost exotic look.

Jorund's heart stopped then started again with a loud thud. It was at this moment that he knew he would never be able to deny her anything. "Is it worth going on for?" he asked, his voice little more than a whisper.

She nodded her head yes.

He took a deep breath before continuing. "We will keep looking, but I will carry you. Do not try to argue. I know you are in pain, I can see it on your face."

She started to protest, but the look on his face stopped her.

"Fine, there is no time to argue anyway. It will be dark soon." She relaxed in his arms and they were both quiet as he continued up the incline.

Asta's side was throbbing at the same pace as the pounding in her head. She relaxed deeper into Jorund's chest as he made his way to the top.

She hated being dependent on a man. She had seen over the years how it could tear a woman up and drag her down to the greatest depths of sorrow. To never be able to do what she wanted or go where she pleased. Having to ask the man for anything she needed or desired. She never wanted to be like that.

Asta had been lucky growing up. Her father, Jarl, had loved his wife, Eriel, and would do anything for her. On her death bed, Eriel had made Jarl promise to protect Asta and teach her to fight like a warrior. This was unheard of, for women were not to fight, only men. But true to his word, Jarl taught Asta everything he knew. He trained her hard, never letting up on her, making her feel all the pain so she would hate it and never want to feel it again. She had learned quickly and soon became better than any man Jarl had trained, except one.

"Am I hurting you?"

The sound of Jorund's voice snapped her out of her reverie. He had stopped walking and was looking down at her.

"No, I'm fine."

"You were tensing up and I thought perhaps I was holding you too tight."

"Let's keep going, we're almost there."

Holding me wrong? How can he think he is holding me wrong when everything about him is so right? She thought, trying hard to keep her eyes ahead of her. She could hear his heart beating under his shirt, smell the salty ocean on his skin, and feel the way his arms held her perfectly to him.

She willed her body to relax. The feelings he invoked in her were unwanted and she needed to get away from him. But she was not naïve. She was weak and knew she would never make it without his help. So she kept her mind focused ahead on the task she was here for.

The next mark was at the top of the hill, the path leading through a space between several large rocks and down a tree-covered slope on the other side. At the bottom awaited their next sign. They moved west through the forest until they came upon two sticks crossed together hanging from a tree.

"This is it." Asta slid from his arms, clenching her jaw as she put her feet on the ground. The pain was almost too much so she turned to hide her face.

Jorund hesitated a moment before dropping his hand from her waist. She slowly walked away hoping to put some distance between them. She had been around men all of her life and none had ever made her feel the way he did.

"What exactly are we looking for?"

Asta walked a few feet and stopped to look around. The cliff ahead of them reached high into the sky and stretched out farther than she could see. "It's not what, but who."

She heard a loud thump behind her. When she turned around Jorund was crumpled on the ground. Above him stood a small woman, her white hair glowing in the fading sun.

"Oh Phaedra, what have you done?" Asta moved to Jorund as fast as she could and kneeled down next to his limp body. She turned him on his back so he was facing her and saw the lump on his head that was already turning purple.

"How nice to see you missed me so much. I've been doing great out here by myself wondering if something happened to you, and you're welcome for saving you from some crazy, gorgeous man who was sneaking up on you," Phaedra spit out, dropping the large piece of wood she still held.

"I did miss you, but he's not some crazy man. He was helping me find you." The sun was fading fast and Asta knew it wasn't safe to be out here in the dark. "We need to get undercover and then I will explain everything. Where have you been staying?" Asta knew Phaedra well enough to know she had scouted out miles of the forest and had found a safe haven.

"There's a cave in the rocks hidden by the ivy," Phaedra answered, pointing toward the high cliff.

"You will have to help me get him there." Asta stood and gripped him under the arms as Phaedra took hold of his feet.

They said nothing as they half-carried half-dragged Jorund to the cave. Once they were inside, they settled him close to the wall on a blanket Phaedra had acquired. The fading sun thrust the cave into darkness. A light burst from the other side of the cave as Phaedra lit a candle, illuminating the dark space enough for Asta to make her way to where her friend sat. She could feel the wetness of the bandage at her side, but she needed to get things in order before she could rest.

"Where is it?"

Phaedra gave her the cloak.

Asta took off the cloak she was wearing and replaced it with her own. She reached into the deep hidden pocket, pulling out the thick gold disc. The round medallion fit perfectly into the palm of her hand and she stared at it, almost hypnotized by the brilliant emeralds that were scattered over its surface. Though she had seen it several times, each time took her breath away.

She sat next to Phaedra, reaching into the bag she had dropped there, and pulled out the chunk of bread. Unwrapping it, she handed the bread to Phaedra then took the cloth and placed the disc inside, wrapping it tight. She shoved it back into her pocket and watched as Phaedra broke the bread and gave a chunk to Asta.

"I think you need to tell me what happened to you, Asta, and tell me who he is." Phaedra quickly ate her piece then sat back waiting to hear from Asta.

"His name is Jorund. He shot me," Asta said, glancing toward Jorund's sleeping form. There was a moment of silence before she turned her attention to Phaedra's shocked face.

"What do you mean he shot you?"

Asta pulled back her cloak and shirt, revealing the bandage that now had a few spots of blood visible. "It was an accident. I went looking for the stones that morning and he happened to be hunting. I walked into his arrow's path." She pulled her cloak tight around her to block the chill from the cave and began nibbling on her meal.

"So why bring him with you?"

"I had no choice. He followed me. It was him and his mother, Dania, who took care of me. It seems I almost died from infection and fever. When I decided it was time to leave, Dania wasn't too excited about the thought. She sent him to escort me, though I think it was just as much his idea as it was hers."

"Then at daybreak we can part ways with him. I wasn't sure what had happened to you so I made my way to the village on the other side of the cliff. We can get passage—"

"No, we need to go back with him."

Phaedra stared at her in silence.

"I am still too weak to be traveling, and I feel we would be better protected within the walls of his village. At least until I feel I can travel. Besides, there is something I need to know, and the only way for me to find out is if we are in this village." Asta gave Phaedra the remainder of her bread then sat back against the wall of the cave.

"We have been together a great time, Phaedra, and for you to understand my intentions, you need to hear my story from the beginning."

Phaedra leaned forward, listening intently, as the story she had been waiting to hear spilled from Asta's lips.

"You see, I was born in his village."She said nodding towards Jorund. "The last time I saw my mother was in this forest as she hid me away."

Someone was pounding on the door, waking him from his deep slumber. Jorund tried to open his eyes, but it felt as if they had been sewn shut. Pain shot through his head as he tried to sit up. He laid back down, only then realizing the pounding was coming from his head.

He opened one eye at a time, gritting his teeth against the pain. There was light coming from an opening ahead of him, but not enough to completely see his surroundings. He could see that he was in a cave. The last thing he remembered was watching Asta walk away, then pain erupted through his head and everything went black.

"The pain will ease faster if you don't move around so much."

The voice, strong and bold, echoed off the cavern walls. He slowly turned his head toward the sound but was only met with shadows.

"Where is Asta?" His voice was a husky whisper lost in the dark. The shadows came to life and out stepped the most unusual woman. She was of medium height, petite, with hair braided to her waist that was so blonde it glowed in the darkness. Her skin was pale, her lips pouty, and what he could see of her eyes, they were clear, void of color.

"She will return soon. She went to retrieve some of our hidden belongings." The girl reached around her and pulled out a flask. She took the ties off and handed it to him. "It's just water," she told him, laughing at the doubtful look on his face. "I don't know you well enough to want to poison you."

"So the better we get to know each other, the closer I need to watch you?" he asked, taking a few gulps of the cool liquid before handing it back to her.

"That may be. It depends on you."

Jorund watched as she moved around the cave collecting things and placing them in a bag she carried.

"So you're Phaedra?"

She eyed him warily. "Asta told you about me?"

"No, not exactly. She mentioned your name to my mother." He slowly moved his body into a sitting position. The pain was at his temple, but the pounding was slowly fading. "So how did you two come to know each other?"

There was quiet as Phaedra moved to the entrance of the cave. She stood there for several moments before speaking. "She saved my life. I was stolen from my home at eight years old and made a slave. I was on the sellers' block when she saw me and bought me. There is no telling what would have happened to me if she had not befriended me."

"You have been together since?"

Phaedra turned to him, her arms folded across her chest. "Yes, everyday. I would give my life to protect her, so you can imagine how I have felt these past days not knowing where she was."

"My head feels like a herd of horses has stampeded through it, thanks to you, I'm sure, so yes, I can imagine how you felt." Jorund rubbed at the large knot that had formed on his temple.

"That was an accident." A playful grin appeared across Phaedra's lips.

"You didn't mean to bash me in the head? And what did you hit me with?"

"It was a large branch that had fallen off a tree and, yes, I did mean to hit you. Only for the reason that I thought you were going to harm her."

They heard the rustling of leaves outside before Asta entered. She handed a bag to Phaedra then looked to Jorund.

"How are you feeling?" Asta walked to him, kneeling down and lightly placing her hand on the side of his head.

Jorund's body quivered from her touch but he didn't move away. Her fingers felt so good on his skin that he closed his eyes and concentrated on her touch. She glided her fingertips across the large knot and then around it, caressing his head with a light massage. A low moan escaped from his throat and she stopped her movements.

"I'm sorry. I didn't mean to hurt you. I was only trying to feel how large the bump was." She pulled her hand away and held it up in front of her. "How many fingers do you see?"

"Is this really necessary?" he asked, gripping the wall to steady himself as he stood.

"Is it that hard for you to answer a question?" she asked back, rising with him.

He rubbed his hand across his face. What a stubborn woman, he thought. But if he had any intentions of getting her to go back with him, he needed to comply. He looked at her hand again. "Three," he answered, taking a few light steps to make sure he had his balance. He then walked to the entrance, parted the opening, and stepped out into the sun. He stopped to let his eyes adjust to the light. The sun was high above the trees so he knew it was already half past the day. The girls emerged from the cave, their bags slung over their shoulders, and stood next to him.

"I have left a man at the edge of the forest to await our return." Jorund was prepared for an argument, but none came.

"We should get going then," Asta replied.

As they walked past him he relieved them of their bags, then he stood there for a moment watching them walk away. What an unlikely pair.

One was so small and petite, with the most unique looks. She could belong to this forest, a fairy in her realm. The other was beautiful and graceful, but stubborn and proud. There was something about Asta that made him want to protect her. He felt as if he had always known her, though he knew it wasn't so.

His head was hurting again and he needed time alone to sort out his thoughts, so he kept his distance behind them as they made their way out of the forest.

The way back was much easier and faster. They walked in companionable silence, emerging from the forest as the sun began its descent. Waiting at the side of the road was a large man, his red hair glowing in the sun. There was a smile on his face as he welcomed Jorund, but as he looked past Jorund to Asta a look of bewilderment changed his expression. This was quickly gone as Phaedra came into his view.

"And who is this?" he asked, his eyes never leaving Phaedra.

"Ladies, this is Gunnar, the village healer. Gunnar, this is Phaedra..."

Gunnar walked around Jorund to stand before Phaedra. He lifted her hand to his lips, lingering a moment before letting it go.

"And this is Asta, as I'm sure you remember."

"Oh yes. Our wounded lady." Gunnar bowed to Asta. "You look a bit tired," he said as he studied Asta's face. "Perhaps you would permit me to look at your wounds?"

Jorund turned to retrieve the horses from where Gunnar had tied them. Asta lifted her shirt and the bandage so Gunnar could make a quick exam of the wounds.

"It is holding nicely, but it looks as if the skin is trying to part again. It is red and swollen. Did it bleed some?" Gunnar pulled the bandage down and Asta dropped her shirt.

"A little bit last night."

"It is good you are returning with us. You need more rest."

"I suppose it is good you are around to check on me. Thank you."

"It is Jorund you should be thanking. He has been by your side the entire time."

"So I have been told." Asta watched as he approached with the horses. Why would he care so much for someone he did not know? Perhaps guilt for what he had done to her was so great that helping her was the only way he knew to show amends.

"There's only two horses and we need to get back to the village before dark. We need to pair up."

Jorund was looking to Gunnar but Asta knew he was talking to her. She could see the way Gunnar and Phaedra were stealing glances at each other, so she turned to Jorund and let him help her onto his horse. Within minutes they were all mounted, Jorund fitting closely behind her, and moving toward the village.

"There's something I've been meaning to ask you."

Asta could feel the soft caress of his breath across her cheek as he spoke to her. "What's that?" She didn't want to answer any questions for him, but it was hard to resist his charms.

"What were you doing in the forest alone?"

"Walking." Short and simple answers, that's what she would give him. She would be safe with that.

"Where did you come from?"

"Across the ocean."

"You walked across the ocean?"

"No, we sailed on a boat. It was too far to swim." She heard a deep, exasperated breath from behind her. Good. Maybe he would quit asking so many questions.

And he did.

Neither talked the remainder of the way, and it wasn't long before the first signs of the village appeared. When Asta first left the village, she was so engrossed in finding Phaedra she never looked back. Now as she watched the tower come into view she wasn't prepared for the sight of the landscape before her.

The tower itself was a tall, dark, imposing stone fortress towering up to the sky. Built off the side was a small building, smoke rising from the chimney, and she knew this was the cooking area. Surrounding all of this was a large stone wall blocking the view to anything else that was behind it. The entrance was closed with two enormous iron gates that were locked tight and guarded to prevent intruders.

Below the outside of the wall was the village, its longhouses running the length of the wall and down toward the outer rim of the forest. It was protected by another massive wall, this made of huge logs that ran from one cliff side to the next, cradling all within.

There were two gates to this wall. One was the main gate, the other opening into a large pasture that had been cut out of the forest and fenced to hold the livestock. Beyond this was a beach with more than a dozen ships bobbing in the water, one so massive it engulfed its neighbors.

It was all so breathtaking and so much larger than she could have ever imagined. She watched as the last of the sun's rays washed across the land, casting it in its glow.

"It's amazing, is it not?" Jorund's words, whispered across her neck, sent shivers through her body.

"Magnificent," she whispered back, too entranced with the village to know she was sitting back comfortably against Jorund's chest. Nor did she see the way he looked at her.

"How many ships are yours?"

"The five that are closest to the tower. There are six in all, but my brother takes one every year upon my return."

"Which is the one you will take when you leave?" It bothered Asta knowing that he would leave when the cold came, but why she did not know. She shouldn't even be asking him, for the more she asked of him the more he would ask—and expect an answer from her. But he didn't seem to mind her questions and spoke with great pride when he answered.

"Mine is the first and largest of them all."

She followed his pointed finger to the farthest ship, the large one she had been admiring. "I have never seen anything like it."

"The idea came from my travels. The first idea came when I learned of a ship called a bireme. It is made to accommodate two rows of oarsmen. The Romans have grand merchant ships with high sides. I studied many various forms of ship building from the ancients to the sea rulers today. Once I put these ideas together, I came up with a ship that provides a larger hold, sleeping quarters for the men, and can still maneuver the water in cases of war."

"The Mediterranean people have a unique way of building ships." She studied the shape and design of the ship, but one main part caught her attention the most: The dragon's head at the bow of the ship that she knew all too well to be Norse.

"You're very observant. I didn't know you had travelled so far."

There was silence again. Asta knew she had given too much information and Jorund must have known she would give no more. He continued talking as if there was never any break in the conversation.

"I could show it to you if you like."

"What?" Asta was still thinking about the slip she made and missed what he had said to her.

"The ship, I could show it to you sometime if you like."

"I would like that very much." Another thought crossed Asta's mind. "Who watches over the land when you're not here, your brother or your father?"

It was then she realized she was sitting so close to him. His entire body tensed and she felt every muscle in his chest contract against her back.

"My father is dead. My brother Ranolf returns and stays for the cold season. He takes care of everything while I am gone."

Asta tried to sit forward to put some space between them, but he grasped her around the waist and held her to him, careful not to disturb her wound.

"Sit back and relax. You need the rest."

She relaxed against him, knowing there was no reason to fight. He was much bigger and stronger than her and she would never get away if she did. But the feelings he evoked in her were not good, so she busied her mind with the sights ahead of her.

"What's happening?" Asta asked as they were passing the many encampments that were being set up outside the village. Women were settled near the many fires and aromas of boiling meat wafted up to her. The main village gate was open wide and throngs of people were moving in and out.

"They are here for the festival. They must have arrived this morning."

"What kind of festival?" Asta was relieved to have something to keep her mind busy.

"It's a trade festival. Every year when I return I bring with me merchandise from all over. There's jewelry, spices, silks, and many more exotic items. Then we open the village to neighboring people. They in turn bring their goods and trade them for mine. Some of them will pay instead of trade, but what is traded gets loaded on my ship for exchange in distant lands when I travel."

"Why not sell it all and then buy your merchandise? Why go through all this?"

"I have learned that some people don't want the money but want to possess things no one else has. To answer your second question, the festival provides a common ground for all. We have games of strength and ability for the men. They practice all year round for this hoping to be the best. It keeps them from fighting among each other."

"Do you participate in these events?" she asked, deeply interested in seeing Jorund's skills in battle.

"That would depend."

"On what?"

"On who would be watching me."

The two horses entered the gates, making their way slowly through the crowds. Men and woman bustled around doing their jobs as the children played throughout the village. On both sides of the wide path small wooden stands were being built, and behind each one tent's were being erected to house the merchants and their families. Past this were the longhouses towering high to block any view from unwanted visitors who made it past the gates. To enter the actual village, one had to walk this path until it opened wide on either side. To the right were more longhouses, to the left a large open arena where she could guess the games would be held.

"How long does this festival last?"

"It takes a few weeks to set up, and then it depends on how many men enter the contest. It ends when there is a winner. After that there is a great celebration with drinking, dancing, and food."

"It sounds fascinating." Asta didn't let her excitement escalate. She and Phaedra would be long gone before then.

The pathway ended at the two huge iron gates that protected the tower within. They stopped and waited as the guards opened the gates to admit them. Once inside they dismounted.

Jorund was off the horse first. Reaching up to take Asta down, he grasped her behind the knees and lowered her to the ground. It took her a moment to steady herself and get her balance.

The sun had completely set and the darkness was now lit by the many torches placed throughout the courtyard. Jorund's fingers lingered a bit too long on her waist and she looked to him with a questioning gaze. His eyes were dark and glazed with a golden shimmer in their depths. Her breath caught and her heart beat faster. She looked away and stepped back, severing the connection. Jorund dropped his hands and walked away as his mother was coming toward them.

"Asta, it is so nice to see you came back." Dania embraced her with a welcoming hug as she watched her son enter the tower. "Is everything alright?" she asked Asta, holding her hand tight. "Is he upset I helped you leave?"

"You talked to him before he left. You should know the answer to that."

"He didn't say much. He only asked which way you went then left without saying good-bye."

"I don't think he is upset with you at all," Asta said, squeezing Dania's hand for comfort. "He probably needs to rest his head awhile."

"You know I only meant to protect you, Asta," Phaedra said, defending herself as she stood next to Asta. "I thought he was trying to hurt you."

"Dania, this is Phaedra. Phaedra, this is Jorund's mother."

"What a beautiful creature you are." Dania hugged Phaedra as she had Asta and welcomed her with a smile. She looped her arms through the girls' and led them inside. "So who wants to tell me what happened to my son?"

"Phaedra hit him in the head with a rather big log."

Dania paused for a minute in shock before shrugging it off and continuing into the tower. "He is up and walking so it is no worse than what he did to you."

"Let's remember these were both accidents," Phaedra said.

Dania led them through the tower to the cookery and sat them down then she started moving about preparing food. She placed two platters full of meat and potatoes along with two mugs of ale in front of the girls and urged them to eat, though it didn't take much.

"You two finish here and then go up and get some sleep. You will be staying in the same room as you were before."

"Thank you," they replied in unison.

Dania merely nodded with a smile, picked up another full platter of food, and left the room.

"So what did you talk about?" Phaedra asked Asta, curious to know what was said. "I watched you two and you were obviously interested in whatever he was saying."

"He talked of the ships and the festival."

"That is all? You seemed to be worried quite a few times."

"Only small slips I made. He was so intent on prying answers from me. What of you? What did you talk of?"

"Gunnar only had one question for me. Did I have a man? When I told him no, he continued to praise my unique looks and then go on about his many accomplishments as a healer."

"No questions of where you came from or how you got here?"

"No, none at all."

"Well, it seems he may be smitten with you, Phaedra."

"Then perhaps I will not get bored being here."

They finished their food while conversing on the splendor of the coming festival. When they were done they made their way up to the room, both falling asleep instantly.

"Jorund?" Dania tapped twice on the door before entering the room.

Jorund was sprawled across the huge bed, his hands under his head, his feet crossed at the ankles, staring into the darkness of the room.

"What is it, Mother?"

"I brought you some food." She closed the door, placed the platter on a table, and lit the candle next to the bed. She sat on the edge of the bed mindlessly rubbing her hand across the green silk cover. "How is your head?"

"Fine." He stood up off the bed to pace back and forth in front of the window. The night was cool and a slight breeze floated in off the water below.

"Please do not be upset with me, Jorund. I did not want her to feel like a prisoner."

Jorund stopped pacing and faced his mother. "I'm not upset with you and she's not a prisoner." He walked to his mother and sat down. "There's so much we don't know about her. She won't even give me straight answers. I get so frustrated with her."

"Well, son, she doesn't have to tell us anything. You brought her here after harming her, by accident," she added, seeing the hurt look on his face, "but that doesn't entitle us to answers."

"I know that, but why would she shy away from telling us who she is unless she has something to hide?"

"She may be confused and scared."

"That woman is afraid of nothing."

"What looks to be on the outside is not always the same on the inside. Things have a way of working themselves out. It just takes time…" she paused, placing her palm on his cheek, "…and patience." She kissed his other cheek and left the room, closing the door behind her.

A smile spread across her face as she leaned against the wall. He had said she, not them. Jorund hadn't even mentioned Phaedra, only Asta. Out of all the women in the world he had met, he was attracted to her. Oh, how fate had a way of working.

Dania walked to her room, her mind now busy with the possibility of Asta falling in love with her son.

Jorund stood by the window inhaling the cool ocean air. No matter what he did he could not get Asta out of his mind. It took every ounce of self-control he had not to ravish her as she sat with him on his horse. Then later, as he took her off the horse, he almost made a fool of himself by kissing her ripe lips. He had traveled the world and seen some of the most beautiful women, had been with the most royal of blood, had watched as they danced and enticed the hardest of men into soft, pliant play things. But never in his life had he felt such strong wanting as he did with Asta.

He turned from the window and lay back on the bed thinking of the nights he stayed with her during her fevered state. She had cried out for help, had asked for the pain to stop. What was happening in that mind of hers? Who would hurt her so badly?

If he ever found out, he would be the last person they would see before their death. Is that what she was doing here? Was she running from someone? Could she be running from her man? That thought shook him to the very bone. Anger swept through him at the thought of another man touching her. But what if it was so?

These and many more questions plagued him throughout the night. Finally he willed himself to sleep. But it would be a rough night as images of a blue-eyed temptress filled his dreams.

Asta awoke to the sound of men working in the distance. She opened her eyes to the bright day outside and sat up in bed, noticing the empty cot at the end. Dania had already been here. The windows were open wide and a tray had been left on the table next to the bed. She sipped from the mug, drinking until the water was gone. Then she picked up a small piece of the bread and walked to the window. Her side was extremely sore, so she moved slowly, leaning against the wall for support.

The day was warm and the sky bright blue. She lifted her face to the cool breeze and the warm sun coming through the window. From here she could see not only the ocean but the dock with dozens of men moving about on all the ships unloading cargo for the festival.

Asta's eyes moved of their own volition to the first ship. There were men everywhere, but she instantly found the one she knew.

Jorund's back was to her as he helped the men move some of the larger wooden boxes, so she watched him as he worked and let her eyes roam over his body. His shirt clung to his back, outlining the expanse of his broad shoulders. She closed her eyes and imagined herself back on the horse with him.

She was pressed tightly to him and could feel every movement his body made. His legs as they controlled the horse, his arms as they guided the way. His scent had surrounded her, and for once she had felt safe. She took a deep breath to clear her thoughts and with a slight smile on her lips she opened her eyes. Her heart missed a beat then frantically sped up.

Jorund had turned, his shirt open, showing his massive chest, and was looking straight at her. Her smile faded. How long had he been watching her? He smiled and waved to her. She waved back but didn't smile. She was suddenly very tired. Turning from the window, she made her way back to the bed. A short nap was what she needed and then she would be rested. She curled up on the bed and let sleep take over.

Her eyes were closed, her face tilted to the sky, the breeze washing over her, lifting her auburn curls away from her shoulders. The slight smile only added to the beauty of this sight. Jorund opened his eyes to the rising sun. This image of Asta burned fresh in his mind, making him want her more.

He rose from the bed and dressed then made his way down to the kitchen where he found Dania cooking over the open flames.

"Good morning to you," he said, seating himself on a stool.

"Give me a moment and this will be ready." She smiled up at him then continued cooking.

Within minutes she had placed a platter of eggs, boiled fish, and bread in front of him. "Are you headed to the ships today?" she asked as she moved around the large space preparing more food.

"No. I will be escorting some of the lairds hunting in our forest."

A chuckle came from his mother as she turned to look at him. "I wonder if you can refrain from bringing home any more women."

Jorund pushed his half-eaten plate away from him and stood. "I do not find this situation amusing." With that said he stomped out the door mumbling under his breath. He wasn't angry with his mother but with himself. He was falling hard for a woman he knew nothing about.

Asta stayed in her room the next day enjoying the company of Dania. Phaedra was rarely seen due to the fact that Asta's injury was worsened from the journey.

"We know nothing of these people. One of us has to keep an eye out for anything unusual," Phaedra had explained the past night as she left the room.

And so Asta and Dania had passed the day with games and a brief lesson in weaving. Asta had never learned to weave and quickly found she did not like it. She missed a row for the third time and, frustrated, threw the craft to the floor.

"Did your mother not teach you to weave?" Dania questioned, picking up the pieces and sitting next to Asta on the bed. She noticed Asta's startled face but said nothing as she unwound the tangled strips and began weaving them together. "See, like this."

Asta watched as Dania's fingers moved across the strips, forming the beginning of what would be a small blanket.

"Once you practice it will be easier to do." Dania handed the piece back to Asta and went back to her chair by the window.

They sat quietly for a while both working on their blankets. The sun started to set and the light in the room slowly started to fade. Asta set her blanket aside and leaned back against the pillows. She watched Dania work, the blanket she had started being more than halfway finished.

"My mother died when I was young. I was raised by my father." Asta didn't know what made her tell this to Dania, but it was too late to take it back. She waited for questions she was sure would come, but Dania was silent. She studied Asta for a moment before breaking the silence.

"I'm sorry for your loss." Dania left the chair and went to the bed. She put the blanket Asta worked on in a basket and slid it into the corner. "If you want to practice it will be there." She lit the candles next to the bed. "I'm going to my room to rest for the night. I will see you on the morrow." Dania retrieved her things from the chair and left the room quietly, closing the door behind her.

What was that about? Dania had seemed almost repulsed by the fact that she was raised up by a man. She thought about this for a while but grew tired. She blew out the candles and lay back in the bed. Within minutes she was asleep.

Dania lit the candles next to her bed and began to undress for the night. She could not get her mind off the things Asta had told her. A young girl raised by a man, not a woman? It was no wonder she was so secretive and paranoid.

Dania sat on the edge of her bed, tears misting her eyes. Asta had said she was raised by her father. But Dania knew that he was no father, but rather a Norse brute bent on death and destruction. Her stomach turned at the thought. She knew what it was like to be ruled by a ruthless barbarian; she had been through it firsthand.

Dania was only nine years old when her village was raided by the fierce men that sailed the Mediterranean Sea. Her father was killed instantly, her mother raped and tortured repeatedly before she was burned in her own house. The men that did this were evil marauders who would take anything they could, even young, virginal girls who they could make a fortune from. She had been passed between too many men to keep count, but what they took of her body they could never take from her spirit. Many had come away with scars that would last a lifetime, but never did they give her what she truly craved. Death. That would have been too easy for her, so instead she had been beaten to within an inch of her life and nursed back to health only to have to repeat it again.

But that was then and this was now. She had met the man who took her away from all of that. Jarod had given her a great life and a loving family. Dania wiped the tears from her face and dressed in her nightgown. Though she didn't know exactly what Asta had gone through, she did know it was enough to keep the poor girl scared.

That was something Dania would change, and it would be so much easier now that she knew she had her unsuspecting son to help, for though he hadn't admitted it yet, she could see that he was falling for this mysterious beauty. It was only a matter of time and planning.

It was still dark when Asta arose from the bed. Phaedra was not there, of course; she would not return until sunrise. On the chair by the window was a pair of trousers, boots, and a cloak. She smiled as she dressed, thanking Dania for knowing she would want to get outside. By the time she made her way out of the tower and along the wall, the sun was starting to glow above the horizon. She walked quietly past the longhouses that guarded the back of the tower and started down the narrow path that ran alongside the cliff's edge. Not many knew of this path, for it blended in with the rocky slope of the cliff.

The sun's rays were now spiking across the water, lighting it with an ethereal glow. She followed the path cautiously, making her way around the small stones that had fallen. As she neared the end of the path it rose up level with the land. From here she could see the edge of the forest on the east side of the tower. A large stone monument came into view, and at the foot of the monument stood two women.

Asta stopped and backed her way down the path until she was hidden. She watched for a moment as they talked. The one facing her was an old lady with long white hair carrying a staff. The other's back was to her but she looked vaguely familiar. Suddenly they separated and Asta bowed her head, waiting for a little time to pass before looking back to where they were. Both women were gone.

She waited a moment longer then continued up and on to the flat land. She walked toward the massive stone but stopped in midstride when the words carved into the stone came into view.

Here lie the remains of our lords
In life and our heroes in death
OLAF AND JAROD

She slowly walked closer and could see it was a headstone set behind a small mound. It was flanked by two larger mounds, their headstones carved with more names than she cared to read.

How long she stood there she wasn't sure, but the sun had already started a path across the sky. The tingle up her spine alerted her to somebody's presence. She looked around and saw no one, but years of training had made her senses sharp. Then, as if her mind had conjured it, there she was, coming from the forest behind the monument.

Asta stood there watching as the woman came closer. This was the old woman she had seen earlier. She carried a long, polished walking staff that was as thick as her wrist and taller than she was. She moved swiftly, her long, dark robe blowing with the wind.

Asta was quiet as the lady came to stand beside her. Did she even know she was there? She took the time to study the old woman. Her eyes were white with the exception of the light rings in the middle. This Asta knew was due to blindness. It was only a moment before her question was answered.

"You have been standing here for quite some time, child. Are you curious?"

Asta was stunned that this woman knew she had been here all along. "How did you know?"

"The sound of the wind changes when there is something blocking its path." The woman smiled, showing almost perfect white teeth. She sounded so young, but Asta could clearly see the deep wrinkles below her eyes. "My name is Marynn." She turned toward Asta and offered her hand. It was rough and calloused but gentle as they shook hands.

"I am Asta." She turned once again to the stone.

"So, are you?"

"Am I what?"

"Curious. You must be or you would not have been standing here so long."

"Yes, I am curious. Do you know what happened to these people?" Marynn may just be able to give Asta some answers about these people and that was something she was desperate to know.

"My cottage is through the forest at the stream's bend. It gets lonely and I wouldn't mind the company. Perhaps you could join me for a meal and I could relay it to you."

"You were here when they lived? Did you know them?"

"Yes, I knew them both." Marynn said nothing else and Asta knew she was waiting for her to accept the invitation.

"When would you like me to come?"

A great smile spread across Marynn's face, stretching the wrinkles, but Asta had no time to examine their odd look, for Marynn had slipped her arm through Asta's and was leading her through the forest.

"The stew will be nice and hot and the bread was baked just this morning."

Asta let Marynn guide her through the forest as she rambled on, excited about having Asta for company. Asta could hear the gurgling of a stream in the distance, and minutes later they came into a clearing.

A small stone cottage sat in the middle, puffs of grey rising from its chimney. There were two windows in the front, one on each side of the dark wood door, decorated with flowerboxes of overflowing colors. The shutters were open wide, permitting the aroma of the stew to drift toward them.

Marynn led Asta into the house and sat her at a table near the window then, retrieving a ladle hanging from the wall, she stirred the large iron cauldron of stew that hung over the fire. Asta let her eyes wander over the inside of the cottage. A dark curtain separated the large space into two rooms. It was open halfway, exposing a bed and chest. By the other window was a small sitting room set up almost like a room from the tower. A large wooden bench lined the farthest wall with over a dozen colorful pillows strewn across it. A jar of fresh heather had been placed on a large oak table that sat below the window.

Asta sat back in her chair and watched as Marynn ladled two bowls of stew out of the pot. Her cooking area was clean but crowded with various sizes of bronze and iron pots stacked along the walls. A large wooden cutting block sat next to the hearth with overflowing jars of herbs and bundles of plants set on the shelves above it.

Marynn placed the two bowls on the table along with a few chunks of bread and mugs of ale then sat in the chair opposite Asta. They ate in silence until the bowls were empty. Marynn pushed her bowl aside and sat up straighter.

"It happened three and ten years past…"

Hours had passed by the time Asta made her way back toward the tower. She emerged from the trees, her head still spinning from the story Marynn had told her. All those names on the headstones were people who had been slaughtered, killed in a horrific raid upon the village, only a handful surviving because they were working in the fields too far out for the raiding party to reach. No one knew who was responsible, didn't even know why it had happened.

Asta heard the horse before she saw it. It was coming at her fast with Jorund on its back. His face was strained and she wasn't sure if he was excited to see her or extremely angry. He stopped the horse and dismounted, coming to stand directly in front of her. He stood there for a moment examining her with his eyes, and then he grabbed her by the shoulders, shaking her hard.

"Where have you been?"

Asta pushed at his chest until he stopped, but he did not remove his hands from her shoulders. For some reason Asta could not explain she didn't drop her hands from his chest.

"I wanted to get outside for some fresh air."

"You should have taken someone with you."

"I didn't know I was a prisoner here. I thought I was a guest." Asta tried to back away from him, but he only tightened his grip.

"You're not a prisoner, but you should have at least told someone."

"The sun hadn't even risen when I woke. Everyone was still abed. Who was I to tell?"

"You should have woke me and told me."

Her movements ceased and their eyes locked. Asta was stunned by the angry concern she heard in Jorund's voice.

"I can defend myself." Her words came out in a low rush. She wanted to look away but couldn't. It was his eyes that held her, hypnotized her, with their dark depths of brown and golden bursts of light. The same colors she had seen before, in the courtyard, when she had been sure he was going to kiss her.

So mesmerized was she that she didn't realize how close he was to her until his breath was caressing her lips. His arms encircled her and she let herself be pulled into his embrace, fitting perfectly into the curve of his body. She closed her eyes as his lips met hers. Tiny sparks of brilliant light danced behind her eyelids and for a moment she was lost to the feel of him. Her hands were no longer against his chest but were curled into his shirt.

The kiss started out soft but quickly grew into a demanding need. She tried to reason with herself but her body was taking control of her mind. He placed his hands on her back to urge her closer. That's when reality crept in to her dream-like state.

Asta pushed at Jorund until he released her, then she took a few steps back before her body had time to react again. She watched him as he regained his senses, and trying hard to hide the turbulence inside of her, she put on her calmest expression. "That can never happen again."

"Why?" He took a step closer, but she moved two steps back to keep the distance.

"You know nothing of me."

"So let me know you."

"I cannot."

"I ask again, why? You cannot deny the pull our bodies feel when we are close, the spark when we touch. I know you feel it too."

Asta couldn't deny it, and as much as she wanted to give her body to this man, she knew it was too dangerous. With a heavy heart she began to tell him the lie that she knew would turn him away.

"I will admit I enjoyed it." The light in his eyes almost stopped her from speaking the rest, but she knew she had to, "but nothing more than the others who have done the same."

She watched as the light faded from his eyes and she had to squeeze her hands into tight fists before she reached out to him.

He turned from her and made his way toward the burial mounds, exclaiming over his shoulder, "Ride the horse back. I will return later."

Asta stood there watching him walk away. Never had a man made her feel so strange inside. She wanted to reach out to him, hold him, and tell him she would stay with him if that's what he wanted. But it was too dangerous. She knew the consequences of love, had seen it firsthand. How many men had she watched die to save their families only to have their families die too? No, she would not bring that upon this man or his people. They have seen enough death for a lifetime and she knew, eventually, her past would catch up with her.

Asta started on the path that led to the village gates, passing his horse on the way. Her legs were weak from the kiss, but she refused to take his horse. Besides, she needed to walk to clear her head of the fog he had caused.

Before turning the bend along the wall, she stopped to look back. Jorund stood at the foot of the monument, head bowed. That was his father, and she knew from what Marynn had told her that they had been close. Asta took one last look at him before turning and moving on.

It wasn't long after Asta entered the village that her mind became distracted from thoughts of Jorund. Having just learned from Gunnar that her son had seen Asta outside the village, Dania was now bustling down the road toward the gate. When she spotted Asta she rushed toward her and hugged her tightly. Hooking their arms together, Dania led her back to the tower explaining on the way how they had all been worried about her. But Asta was only vaguely aware of what Dania was saying. She was too caught up in the activity around her.

Men and woman were unloading their merchandise for display at the stands. Beads of several colors were being set out for purchase along with gold, silver, and bronze jewelry. Other merchants were selling food, silks, dishes, and even a gypsy with her fortune telling was trying to sell her gift of seeing the future.

They moved past the stands to the open arena. The large platform for seating was finished and standing grand on one side and a smaller was being built next to it. Large black tents had been set up on the far side and dozens of men were moving in and out of them, some emerging with bare chests.

"What are they doing?"

Dania looked to where Asta pointed. "They are practicing for the games. Each tent contains two obstacles. Only eight men are allowed in a tent at a time." Dania pointed to a line of men formed behind the farthest tent. "They are all waiting for a turn."

"There are so many."

"That is only half of the men that will participate."

They continued on into the tower gates where Asta spotted Phaedra talking to Gunnar. The moment she saw Asta, she whispered to Gunnar and he glanced their way. Phaedra started toward them with a wide grin on her face.

"I told them that they worried for nothing." Phaedra said, hugging Asta. "I knew you would go crazy inside and would wander off when you were feeling right."

Asta could tell something was amiss with her friend. She could see the troubled look in her eyes.

"I went to see the sunrise from the cliff. I walked a bit and came upon the burial mound to the east of the village. It was there I met the most unusual woman. She invited me to eat and I accepted."

"It's so nice that you have been welcomed by the villagers," Dania said, smiling broadly.

"She does not live in the village but out by the stream. Her name is Marynn."

Danias eyes were wide with shock, her mouth slightly open. "You met her?"

"Yes. Is something wrong?"

The smile was back on Dania's face, but Asta could still see the panic in her eyes. "Not at all, she is just a very private person and I didn't expect you to meet so soon. Now if you will excuse me, I have things to attend to." With that said, Dania spun on her heel and walked away, leaving Phaedra and Asta alone.

"We need to talk." Phaedra made her way through the tower and to their room with Asta following behind. Once inside Phaedra closed the door then joined Asta on the bed. "I need to tell you what has taken place while you were out making a friend." Phaedra stood and paced back and forth before Asta.

"What is it, Phaedra? You look as if you've seen a ghost."

"It was not me who has seen it. Let me go back a few days. Angus McGregor is the village blacksmith. Two days ago a man came to him curious about what was taking place here. When Angus explained the festival the man became angry. He then insisted that Angus shine and sharpen his sword even though it was already perfect. The man stayed outside the entire time leaning against the wall watching every person that passed by, as if he was looking for someone particular."

"There are people coming and going all the time. Why would this man be any different?"

"The people are here for the festival. This man knew nothing of it." Phaedra sat back down and took Asta's hand. "That's not all. This morning his son Ian was out in the pasture with his sheep. He heard a strange noise but the fog was too thick for him to see, so he blindly made his way toward the sound. Seconds later he heard the sound of horses riding away. He looked to the hill that led to the forest and saw three men riding away. One man turned to look back at the tower, one of Ian's sheep slaughtered and draped across his horse."

"The men were stealing sheep?"

"It's not about the sheep, Asta. Ian described this man. He said he wore all black, his horse was all black, but his hair was white, glowing in the sun like a shiny crown." Phaedra sat quietly still holding Asta's hand and waited for a reaction. It was a long minute before realization dawned in Asta's eyes. A deep shudder ran visibly through her body.

"How did he find us?" Asta's voice was low but almost hysterical.

"He did not find us. If he knew for sure we were here he would not have left without us."

"What if he didn't leave but waited for us? All these people could be in danger."

"They would not let anything happen. The village is well guarded."

"They may be able to defend the tower, but what of the people in the village and beyond. If he was so easily let into the village then there could be others here as well."

"Calm yourself, Asta. Jorund took some of his men and rode out through the forest beyond the pasture. They found an encampment that had been abandoned. The fire pit was warm but dying so they had probably been gone for hours. They found the sheep carcass but it had been cleaned of the meat and hung in a tree."

"That sounds like him, always hanging the remains of dead in the trees."

"Jorund was already upset when he came back without the thieves, but when no one could find you he completely lost control. He went over the entire village looking for you when a woman outside the village spotted you emerging from the forest."

So that's why Jorund was upset. He was worried about her. That thought unnerved and excited Asta.

"What are you smiling about? This is not good news." Phaedra was clearly agitated with Asta's sudden lack of concern.

"If he's gone then he has no reason to suspect we are here. He wouldn't have left without us, you said it yourself. He's probably moving from village to village trying to find information."

"What if he has left someone here to spy?"

"If he did, it would take a while for that person to find him and even longer for him to make his way back here. We should be safe enough until we leave."

"When is that going to be?"

"As soon as I feel sure I can travel without hindering our way."

"So you have found what you wanted to know?"

"Yes, though I am not happy with the answers."

"So tell me what you have learned."

"Marynn has lived here a long time, even before what the villagers call the massacre. She told me of the raid and how Jorund and his family were on their way but arrived too late. It was Jorund who found the heads of his father Jarod and the laird Olaf on pikes at the cliff's edge. To this day no one knows what happened to the laird's wife or daughter. No bodies were ever found."

"So now you know how they came to be here."

"The only thing I don't know is why. Marynn said something about Jarod travelling for hours from his home to get here before his wife and children. He was to greet some new found family. That may be why the village wasn't prepared to defend themselves. Even the laird and his wife were taken by surprise." Asta stood from the bed and walked to the window.

"So why was Dania acting so strange?" Phaedra spread out across her cot, tucking her hands under her head.

"I don't know. Perhaps she is afraid of what Marynn will tell me, afraid it will scare me away, though she must know we will leave soon anyway."

Asta sat in the chair near the open window and let the breeze wash over her face. She looked out over the ocean, watched the waves grow bigger the closer they came to land, then disappear before she heard them crash into the cliff below.

Asta sat quietly absorbing all that had happened, but one thought was invading her mind. Jorund. His touch, his scent, his taste. The memory of that moment when he took her into his arms and kissed her rushed overwhelmingly over her. She closed her eyes and took a few deep breaths to calm her rapid heartbeat. Every time Jorund came close to her she had no control over her body's reaction.

She stared back out over the ocean. It would never happen for them. If he knew the truth about her, he would never want to see her again. She looked to the docked ships, spotting Jorund instantly. He was unloading barrels and crates from the ships and carrying them into the village. She watched him until he disappeared beyond the wall, then she sat back in the chair, only then realizing she had been leaning forward to see him.

"Damn him!" she hissed, leaving the window and walking to the bed. Why did he have to kiss her and make her feel this way? She glanced down at Phaedra but she was fast asleep.

Asta lay across the bed and closed her eyes, but his image was still there haunting her thoughts. She shook her head trying to clear her mind. It would do her no good to think of things that could never be. Instead she thought back to the beginning. What a cruel game fate played. She wondered if, even now, the goddesses were planning more destruction in her life. This was her last thought as she fell into sleep.

He knew it had to be her, but he needed to be sure. He had been waiting all day for her to emerge from the tower gates, but with no luck. He thought he had seen her at one point entering the gates, but he was too distant to be sure. Now, here it was night, the last of the sun's ray's slipping behind the horizon. It was time to put another plan into action. Tomorrow he was to leave and he did not want to be the bearer of bad news. He slipped into the forming shadows and made his way toward the ships. He waited until late into the night when everything was quiet to begin.

It was dark, pitch black. Asta stumbled across the floor feeling her way around the room, but there was nothing there. Panic and fear gripped her. Out of the dark came light, golden sparks that lit the room with warmth. It was Jorund coming to save her. He wrapped his arms around her and kissed her deeply, and then he trailed kisses down her neck and back to her waiting lips. But when she pulled back to look at him it wasn't Jorund at all. The same golden eyes were there, but it was a different man that held her. She screamed and fought against his hold.

Asta sat up in the bed struggling with the covers. She unwrapped herself from the blanket and kicked it to the floor. She stayed where she was letting her mind adjust to reality. The room was dark with only a sliver of moonlight to light the room. As her eyes adjusted she could see Phaedra's cot was empty. She moved to the edge of the bed and removed the shoes she still wore, then she walked to the door and slowly opened it. It must be late for there was no noise coming from the tower. She closed the door and made her way to the window, opening it wide to permit more light.

On the side table next to the bed sat a tray of bread and cheese and next to that a mug of ale. She took a few bites off the tray and a sip of the drink then unbraided her hair and stood by the window combing her fingers through it.

A movement caught her eye down by the ships. She looked over the dark masses trying to pinpoint where it had come from, but all was quiet and nothing moved. She continued combing the knots from her hair when she saw it again. She braced herself on the window's ledge, leaning forward for a better look. She could barely make out the cloaked figure that was crouched on one of the ship's decks. Suddenly he stood and ran from the ship, but she did not see where he went, for her gaze was focused on the flames that were now moving across the deck. She ran to the door and flung it open.

"Fire!" she screamed as she ran to Dania's door then to Jorund's. "The ship is on fire." She pounded on Jorund's door a second time before turning to go. Halfway down the stairs she heard Jorund's mumbled curses as he opened his door. She turned around but was struck speechless as she gazed at his half-naked torso.

"What is all the noise about?"

She snapped out of her daze and started down the stairs again telling him over her shoulder, "One of the ships is on fire."

By the time she reached the bottom of the stairs she could hear Jorund throw open his window and head down the stairs himself. Within seconds he was in the great hall waking all his men then running out the door ahead of her.

She followed behind him along with the crowd that was rapidly growing. She could see the smoke rising in great puffs beyond the wall, but nothing could have prepared her for the forthcoming chaos she was about to enter.

As she approached the beach she could feel the flames of the now massive fireball that had once been a grand ship. Men were running onto neighboring ships trying to douse the small flames that were jumping from the burning timber. A dozen men, including Jorund, used long poles to push the blazing ship away from the shore and out into deeper water. Then Jorund made his way onto one of the other ships to help with the fires that had spread there. She started toward the ships, but a firm hand grasped her by the arm.

"It is best if you let them do this." Dania dropped her hand from Asta's arm.

"I can't stand here and do nothing."

"If you go out there those men would be distracted. They may hurt themselves worrying over you."

"Why would they worry over me?"

Dania linked arms with Asta and led her back to the tower. "Because they are men, they feel a strong urge to protect that which is important to them."

"Not all men find women important."

Dania squeezed Asta's hand. "You have been around the wrong men."

The sun was now rising and the men could be heard gathering in the courtyard. Asta watched as the women took platters of food away to pass out to their tired heroes. She overheard the conversation of two younger girls who were heading to the courtyard with platters laden with food.

"Thank the gods for the rain. Every ship could have been destroyed."

"Five ships felt those flames, only one was destroyed. I would say that's something to be thankful for."

Asta finished slicing the last of the bread, washed her hands in the water basin, and discarded her apron. "Can I help with anything else?" she asked, sitting on a stool next to Dania.

"No, dear, you were very helpful, but you look tired. You should go rest now."

Asta was exhausted, her side aching with each minute that passed, but the vision of the cloaked figure invaded her mind, keeping her nerves on edge. "I would rather stay and help, if you don't mind. I couldn't sleep right now if I wanted to anyway."

"Of course I don't mind." Dania waited for the last of the women to leave then turned to Asta. "It is you we should be thanking. If you hadn't seen that fire we would have lost everything."

"Am I intruding or can I get some of that food I see everyone devouring?" Jorund was leaning in the door, arms crossed, a grin across his dirt-streaked face. He was covered in ash and soot, but even this only added to his sexy appeal.

"You're not intruding at all." Dania prepared another platter as Jorund sat on the stool she had occupied.

"I was telling Asta how grateful we are that she saw the fires and woke us." Dania placed the food in front of Jorund along with a mug of ale, then she excused herself so she could check to make sure all the men had been fed.

As soon as she disappeared through the doorway, Jorund put his mug down and turned to Asta.

"Care to tell me how, exactly, you knew of the fire?" He sat back, arms crossed, waiting for her answer.

"I woke up late in the night. I opened the window for some air and saw something moving. At first it was so slight I didn't think anything of it, but then it was there again."

"What was there?"

"It was a figure wearing a dark cloak. He ran off and that's when I realized the ship was on fire."

"Did you see who it was?"

"I told you he was wearing a dark cloak."

"Which way did he go?"

"I didn't see."

"Let me get this straight. You were up that late at night and just happened to be looking out the window. You saw a figure moving about the ship, even saw the flames, but you didn't see who it was or which way he went?" Jorund uncrossed his arms and leaned toward her. "Two of my guards were knocked unconscious and five ships were damaged. I want to know exactly what it was you saw."

Asta couldn't believe what was happening. He was acting as if she had something to do with the fire. "I told you, I couldn't sleep so I went to the window for some fresh air."

"Why couldn't you sleep? Were you dreaming?"

"What?"

"You said you couldn't sleep. Why, nightmares?"

Asta's control slipped for only a moment, but it was long enough for Jorund to see he had hit the mark.

"That has nothing to do with what has happened."

"You are the only witness, so I would say it has everything to do with what has happened. Who were your nightmares about, Asta?"

"What I dream is none of your concern." She rose from the stool. "I have told you everything I know." She ground out between clenched teeth, "Now, if you will excuse me."

"If I don't you will leave anyway."

She walked past him to the door just as Dania was entering.

"Going to rest?"

"Yes, I am suddenly quite tired." And then she was gone.

The man huddled deeper into the crowd. From where he was positioned he had a clear view of the petite blond. He knew this was the companion of the woman he looked for. She had the unique look of a magical forest creature, a fairy, just like he had been told. If he waited long enough he would see the one he searched for.

A few minutes later his patience paid off. She was standing in the tower door, her auburn hair shining in the sun. Her eyes quickly scanned the crowd, stopping when she spotted who she was looking for. The large man talking to the blond said something to her and the woman turned to see her friend beckoning to her. Together the two women entered the tower.

He was positive it was her. He came out of his spot and pushed through the crowd. If he rode fast he could catch his master within the week. He walked to his tent and, without packing a thing, mounted his horse and left.

"What did you say to her?" Dania sat on the stool next to Jorund. His untouched food had been pushed to the side and he drank heavily from the second mug she had brought him.

"I only meant to get her to open up to me, tell me some answers."

"I told you to give her some time. She will come to trust us, but it has to be of her own will, not because you want it."

"But can we trust her? There's something she's hiding. She will talk to me, but when she says too much or sees my interest, she puts a wall up."

"With that frown on your face I can see why. You probably frighten her."

"She seems to be fearless."

Dania walked to her son and placed a kiss on his cheek. "No one is completely fearless. Now go get some rest. There will be plenty to do later and you will need your strength."

She watched as Jorund climbed the stairs. Everyone departed to their homes for the day except the few women who were cleaning up the leftover food. Dania took off her apron, hung it on a hook, then she left the tower and walked through the village. There was an old friend she needed to see.

"I cannot believe he dared ask me such questions. It sounded to me like he thought I had something to do with the fires."

"You may have misunderstood him."

Asta stopped at the door to their room and glared back at her friend. "I heard what he said loud and clear."

They entered the room, Phaedra closing the door behind her.

"Where were you anyway? You didn't see anything unusual?" Asta asked as she shed her trousers and climbed into the bed.

Phaedra lay across her cot, propping herself on her elbows so she could see Asta. "I saw no one other than the night guards walking through the village as usual."

"Someone set that fire. That I know for sure. We can't rule out the fact that it may be one of Jorund's enemies or a visitor's."

"With everything that has happened and the fact that we are running from someone who is evil beyond this world, do you actually believe it had to do with someone other than ourselves?"

"I was only saying it was a possibility."

"I think we should tell them the truth."

"And what should I tell them? My family slaughtered your people? Would that be a good way to start?"

"That's not the truth, Asta."

"It might as well be. I was raised by them, Phaedra, for more years than not. How am I to forget that when they are the reason I am me?"

Phaedra was now looking down, plucking at her blanket with her fingers. "They have been so nice to us. If they knew they may be able to help us."

"May I remind you it was Jorund who shot me and almost brought me to my death?"

Phaedra looked back at Asta. "It was an accident, you said so yourself."

"Yes, that was, but that was not the first time I have been close to death and those were not accidents. Do not forget who we are, Phaedra. We are killers of men, women, and even children. We have seen rape, torture—"

"Stop! That was for survival, not for the pleasures the other men sought."

"We had a choice."

"And our choice was to give them a swift death. You know the pain that would have been inflicted on them by those savages you call family." The tortured look on Asta's face broke Phaedra's heart. Though Asta had never mentioned it, Phaedra knew how much she longed for a family of her own. "I think if we told Dania and Jorund, they would understand."

"We cannot take the chance. I only need a bit longer to heal then we will be on our way. You did not forget why we came here, did you?" Asta could see by the look on Phaedra's face that she had forgotten.

"Maybe it's time to put the past where it belongs, behind us."

Asta lay down with her back to her friend. "I will never forget."

There was silence for a moment before Phaedra spoke. "Asta?"

"Go to sleep, Phaedra."

"I'm sorry, Asta."

"I know. Now go to sleep. I'm tired." Asta lay there listening to Phaedra settle into her bed. It wasn't long before Asta could hear her steady breathing. She was asleep.

Asta rolled onto her back and stared above her. She had been seeing Phaedra less and less since their arrival and she knew it had to do with a man. It had come to Asta's attention the day she had meant Marynn. As she and Dania entered the tower gates, she noticed Phaedra with her fingers placed lightly on Gunnar's arm as she smiled up at him. Asta had almost stumbled. She had never seen Phaedra glowing, happy, and in love.

Her mind flipped back through the past to the first time she had met Phaedra.

Asta was travelling with her father and his men on the Pnieper River to Byzantium. They had stopped at a small town to rest. It was here, in the market place, where Asta had spotted her. She was a young, small waif of a girl with crystal blue eyes and hair to match her pale skin. She was being sold as a slave as were many young girls throughout the town. The man bargaining for her was fat, dirty, and slovenly dressed. Asta could see that he had different thoughts than to use her as a servant by the way he rubbed his grubby hands together. She could not let that happen.

Asta made her way through the crowd of people to the girl.

"How much do you want for this one?" Asta asked without looking away from the girl.

"She's already sold."

"I will give twice what he is offering." Asta glared at both men when their laughter split the air. "This is funny to you? You do not want the payment I am offering you?"

The thin, toothless man who was selling the girl laughed harder, but the other man stepped closer to Asta.

"And where would the likes of you get money like that?" He looked her up and down. "You can't even afford to wash."

"I could say the same for you. My uncleanliness is from days of travelling. What excuse do you have?"

"Look here, girl..." The man started reaching out toward Asta.

His hand stopped midway, but she kept the pressure of her blade against his throat in case he changed his mind.

"I would like to be civilized about this. It is business and nothing more. But if you choose it to be otherwise, know that I will slice you from ear to ear. Do you understand?"

He hesitated for only a moment before nodding his head and backing away into the crowd.

"Girl, you best have payment for me." The toothless man was approaching her pulling the girl behind him.

Asta reached to her side, cutting the smallest bag from her belt. She handed it to the man and reached for the child. He opened the pouch and poured it into his hand. A few red rubies shone among the small pile of gold coins. "This will do nicely." When he looked up the girls were gone.

Asta rolled onto her side and looked toward the open window. Good-byes were hard, but this is how it had to be. She just wished it wasn't so soon. With the crash of the waves and the cool breeze blowing through the window, it wasn't long before she drifted to sleep.

Jorund's mood only worsened with the passing day. After a few hours of restless sleep, he made his way to the beach to assess the damage done to the ships. One had been lost, but only two of the others damaged needed major repairs. Tensions were high and he knew fingers would start to point if he didn't calm the situation.

He told no one of the conversation he and Asta had had that morning. The knowledge that someone had set the fire would surely bring the want of retaliation among the people. And since they did not know who had done it, every visiting villager would be blamed, fighting would break out among the people, and there would be many deaths. So to keep the violence from occurring, he offered one of his smaller boats to the laird who had lost his and helped to repair the others. But still this caused a problem.

"We are still in need of a working boat. There are goods we have yet to bring here from the island." Laird Droch was ruler of the northern islands and one of the many lairds who had at first scoffed at the idea of a trade festival. But many visits and hard talks had brought him around to the idea. Peace was better than death. His was one of the ships they now worked on repairing.

"It would be my pleasure to assist you." Jorund offered his personal ship to help finish transporting the goods, and since he was captain, he was to set sail day after next.

For the remainder of the day he helped remove debris from the decks of the damaged ships as his men prepared his ship for sailing. This did not keep Asta from his thoughts. He was constantly looking to her window waiting for her to appear as she so often had. Today she never did.

When the sun started to set he made his way back to the tower. He wanted to apologize for his words to Asta this morning. He was stopped by Gunnar who was descending the tower stairs.

"Is everything alright?"

"Yes, it's fine. I was checking Asta."

"How is she faring?"

"Good, but she will need a day of rest."

Jorund moved past Gunnar and headed up the stairs.

"If you're on your way to see her I will let you know she is sleeping."

Jorund ignored his friend and made his way to her room, knocking softly.

Phaedra slipped out, closing the door behind her. "She's sleeping. Gunnar has given her something so she may rest."

"I was hoping to talk to her."

"All the panic and running around has put a strain on her wounds. Gunnar told her she needed to rest if she was to get better."

Again he was stricken hard by the guilt he had been harboring since bringing her here. All the pain and suffering she had endured was his fault and his alone.

"It will do no good for you to care for her as you do."

Jorund was surprised by the force and the truth of Phaedra's words. He did care for Asta, more than he should. Every day that passed his feelings grew for her, but at the back of his mind was the heaviest reminder of why it could never be. Her secrets. But that didn't explain Phaedra's comment. Jorund narrowed his eyes toward her.

"Why is that? Does she have a man?"

Phaedra covered her mouth to stop a burst of laughter. "No, she has no man, and she does not want one, ever."

"Why? Has she been hurt by a man?"

All traces of laughter disappeared from her face. "She has seen what men can do and has vowed to never let a man control her."

"What has she seen?"

There was silence for a brief moment before another smile lit Phaedra's face. "Jorund, I believe you are trying to get me to tell you things that are not mine to tell." Phaedra walked past him but turned back before descending the stairs. "You could ask her."

"I have tried. She will not give me straight answers."

"Before asking your question, be sure of what it is you ask. She has a way of turning things around so it is you answering her questions."

"Yes, I have noticed." It only took a moment for the idea to come to his mind. "I know you're her friend and I am the last person you should be helping, but I very much want to talk with her, get to know more about her."

"What is it you want from me?"

Jorund placed his arm around Phaedra's shoulder. "I knew I could count on you. Now, I was thinking..."

"Asta!"

Someone was violently shaking her out of her deep slumber.

"Asta, wake up."

Asta opened her eyes to the sun that was still rising. She rolled over to find Phaedra standing next to the bed.

"Jorund wants to show you the ships, if you're interested. He needs to check the repairs to the two ships damaged and said you wanted to see his ship."

"Repairs, so soon? Does the man not sleep?" Asta replied, sitting up on the edge of the bed and wiping her hand across her face.

"Not as long as you. I tried to wake you twice yester eve. You woke only once complaining of the pain in your side so I had Gunnar look you over and give you something to sleep."

Asta's hand dropped to her side. "I slept all day and night?"

"Yes." Phaedra talked as she gathered Asta's clothes and placed them on the bed. "They started cleaning up the debris at noon yesterday." She turned toward the door to leave. "There's fresh water behind the screen. Now hurry up. We will be waiting in the hall."

"We?"

"Yes, we," Phaedra said over her shoulder. "I was invited too." She left the room, closing the door behind her.

Asta stood, slowly stretching her arms above her head. When the pain was too much, she lowered them to her side and lifted her shirt to examine the wounds. They were still red but no longer swollen.

She went to the window, inhaling deeply to wake herself. Something bothered her about this excursion. Why would Jorund want to show her his ship after the implications he made to her about the fires? And why would he invite Phaedra along knowing she would be on Asta's side?

She watched the men working on the ships. The last thing she wanted was to spend even a moment in Jorund's company, but her curiosity was overwhelming. She carried the trousers and shirt Phaedra had left out for her to the screen and, with a shake of her head, went about her morning ablutions.

As Asta descended the stairs she heard loud voices and laughter echoing through the tower. She stopped after the first few steps to listen to the group below.

"I told her not to, but she insisted on knocking it down. The next thing I know, she's running by me swinging her arms like a mad woman and jumps into the river."

A deep laugh rang out above the rest. Never had she heard Jorund laugh. Smile, yes, all the time, but never laugh. She continued down the stairs scanning the crowd as they came into view.

Dania stood at the cookery door looking at the small crowd, two young maidens by her side. Phaedra stood next to Gunnar who was seated at the large table at the forefront of the great hall. She was telling her story to a smiling Jorund, who was seated across from Gunnar, and a small boy who was seated next to him. A large man stood behind the young boy, his hand resting protectively upon his shoulder.

"You may be laughing now, but at the time it wasn't funny at all."

All eyes turned to Asta as she reached the bottom of the stairs and came to stand next to the table.

"Were you stung very badly?" Jorund asked, never looking away from her.

"Not as much as Phaedra, but I became very ill for days after."

"Phaedra was stung by the bees? I thought you were the one that knocked the hive from the tree?" Gunnar asked Asta, but it was Phaedra who answered.

"She did, but in her haste to get to the river she ran too close to me. The bees began swarming around me."

"And she ended up in the river with me." Asta found herself smiling as the laughter filled the room.

"Asta, I don't believe you have met Angus." Jorund introduced her to the large man.

Asta smiled and shook his hand.

"This is his son Ian."

Asta gave the boy the same smile. He smiled back, rising from the table, ushered the others to follow, and left the tower.

"He's eager to see the ships." Angus said, following his son.

Gunnar and Phaedra left next, leaving Asta and Jorund to follow behind them. Outside the sun was shining, the earth was warming, and people were moving around preparing for the day. Up ahead she could see Ian skipping along the path.

"Does he talk much or is he just shy?"

"He hasn't said one word since his mother's passing."

"They must have been close."

They walked in silence as Asta took the time to look over the arena. Many workers hustled about and men who had joined the games practiced their sport. The path they were on ran along the outer tower wall, but they were now behind the large stands that had been built to seat the many spectators that would be there to watch the men battle. They continued on passing the training tents where a line of men was rapidly growing, past the village houses, and closer to the beach before Jorund finally spoke.

"Ian watched his mother throw herself from the high cliffs."

Asta knew by the look on Jorund's face that he was telling the truth. "How terrible. Why would she do that?"

"She was having an affair with another man. When Angus found out, he confronted the man and challenged him to fight. Angus won."

"What happened to the man?"

"He left the village. After the fight Angus went home and an argument ensued with his wife. She told Angus she never loved him and married him only because she carried his child, a child she never wanted. She admitted to being with child again, but Angus knew this was not his child. Some years before he had been injured and could no longer sire children."

"What happened next?" Asta was so engrossed in the story that she did not think about why they had stopped or the fact that Phaedra looked back smiling but continued on.

"She packed a bag and left, but when she found her lover had left without her, she tried to return to Angus."

"Did he take her back?"

"No, he turned her away. He told her people knew he could not father a child and that he would not be made to look a fool. He wouldn't let her in the house, told her to never come back. Ian was there, he witnessed everything. He followed her out to the cliffs. That's where Angus found him, curled up on the ground, his mother at the rocky bottom below."

"That poor child." Asta looked ahead but saw no one so she began walking again.

"I wanted to apologize," Jorund said, following behind her.

Asta slowed down until he was walking beside her. "Does that mean you don't think I had something to do with the fires?"

"I never did. My words came out wrong. I just thought that you may have recognized the person."

"I told you he wore a cloak."

"And I believe you."

They reached the beach and she followed him onto one of the ships. Almost instantly Jorund began helping with the repairs. The five ships sat in a row, but only two had visible damage. The mast of one had caught fire and the stern had been crushed where it had fallen. The other's deck had been burnt, but now men were pulling the black slats free to be replaced with new ones. There were so many men helping and nothing for Asta to do so she went in search of Phaedra.

Hours later, Asta sat with Phaedra on the sandy beach, both resting from the work of passing out food and drink to the men.

"I could get used to this."

"Get used to what?"

"Letting the men do the work while we only have to feed them."

"You can't mean that. That is the same thing that most of the villages we plundered thought, and look where that left them."

"I didn't say women shouldn't learn to fight."

"If the men do all the work and the women are only here to take care of the men, do you really think the men would let the women learn to fight? No, they would want to control the women and every aspect of their lives."

"You are so bitter, Asta. Not all men are like that. Don't you think there may be a man out there who would love you enough to treat you like an equal?"

"Do you?" Asta watched Jorund as he drank and talked with his men. One of them leaned toward him and said something in a low voice. Jorund's scowling face turned toward her and she quickly looked down at the drink in her hand.

"You should be careful how you watch him else people will start to talk."

Asta sucked in her breath and looked to her friend. "And what would they say?"

"They would say how Jorund has become much moodier since your arrival and how the atmosphere sizzles when you look at one another, though you both try to deny it."

"They would say it, or they do?"

"I think you know the answer to that question."

They sat in silence sipping their drinks. Asta stood and wiped the sand from her trousers.

"You know that it could never be."

"Why? For once follow your heart, Asta. I can see you are starting to care for him. You could be happy."

Asta looked to her friend, eyes ablaze. "I will not put anyone in danger. That is what my heart tells me. You know what happened here before. I will not be the cause of it happening again."

"Tell them, Asta. They will protect you." Phaedra stood to face her friend.

"Are you sure, Phaedra? They are harsh in their belief of revenge on any of the savages—and their kin—who took the lives of their beloved lairds. They even have a festival every year to mark the occasion."

Phaedra gave Asta a questioning look. "This?" she asked, waving her hand toward the village.

"You didn't know? I thought someone would have told you. They claim it to be a trade festival, but Marynn told me it first started out as a celebration to mark the deaths of those lost."

"I didn't know."

"Do you understand why I hesitate to let them know the truth? Do you think they would be so forgiving now?"

Phaedra hesitated before answering. "I don't know."

"And neither do I." Asta hugged Phaedra tight. "For now we need to be on the lookout for anyone who may be suspicious. I will deal with Jorund the best I can."

"I hope you're ready then. Here he comes."

The ship was greater than Asta had anticipated. From a distance it was large enough, but up close the ship was gigantic. It was at least one hundred feet, maybe more, and could accommodate twenty oarsmen per side. It was split into two decks. The lower deck was used as the hold and also housed the men for the long journeys. It also consisted of holes built into the sides for the oars. The top deck had a central mast, huge sails tied down to it, and a large cabin built at the stern of the ship. This was Jorund's room and this was where she stood now surrounded by his personal effects.

One wall was lined with weapons of various sizes. A large oak table, scattered with maps and navigation instruments, sat below them. Two tall chairs of dark wood stood before her, a small table with a jug and two goblets between them. To the other side of the room was a bed. Colorful silks and thick furs were thrown across it along with large, plush pillows similar to the ones in the tower. To each side of the bed hung a long red curtain held back by gold tasseled rope.

A shiver ran along her spine. She should never have come here with Jorund, not alone. She should have made Phaedra accompany her. She turned to leave and found Jorund standing by the door, hands behind his back.

"She… she's beautiful."

"Yes, she is," he replied slowly walking toward her.

She took two steps back before her legs were against the table. He stopped in front of her and reached around her. He was so close she could smell the ocean and scent of wood that lingered on his skin. Her hand instinctively went to the small knife she had stashed under her garments.

"Would you like some wine?" he asked as he turned from her and walked to his desk, the jug from the table in one hand, the two goblets in the other.

"No thank you." She dropped her arms to her side and, letting her body relax, sat down in the chair next to her. She watched as he poured wine into both goblets and then returned, handing one to her.

"Drink. It will help with the discomfort."

Asta wasn't sure if he was referring to the wound or the way he was making her feel, but he was right, she needed it. She accepted the wine and drank the smooth liquid while Jorund, sitting in the chair opposite her, watched. It only took seconds for her to feel the effects. She set the empty cup on the table then sat back in the chair, more relaxed than she had been in a long time, and crossed her arms over her chest.

"So?"

"What?"

"There's obviously something you want to know or you would not be staring at me like that."

"Can I not sit here and admire a beautiful face?"

"I may be young, but I am not stupid nor am I naïve. I can see it on your face. You have many questions, as does everyone else."

"Did you expect less?"

"No, for I am a stranger to you and these people, but let me remind you that it was not my intention to be here."

The smile faded from Jorund's face. He stood, walked to his desk, poured more wine into his goblet, and swallowed in one gulp. She was quiet as he stood with his back to her. It seemed an eternity before he finally turned to her. Though his face showed no emotion she could see the anguish he felt in his eyes.

"You do not have to remind me. I remember each time I see you wince from stretching the wrong way, or how sometimes you limp when it bothers you too much. For this I am truly sorry. Please, tell me you know it was an accident."

She felt the guilt of her words weigh heavy on her soul. She should not have made him feel so terrible for the pain he had caused her. For that he felt bad enough.

"Yes, I know it was an accident. I know you would not have done that purposefully."

He set his cup down and walked to her, pulling her from the chair. "I am sorry for the pain I caused you, but I cannot be sorry for bringing you here, and I am not sorry for this."

When his lips touched Asta's, it was like a lightning bolt streaking through her body. She knew she should stop it now, but her body was overriding her brain. A small moan escaped her mouth, prompting Jorund to deepen the kiss. His hands were roaming her body, down her back to the curve of her bottom and back up again to tangle in her hair. Once his tongue invaded her mouth, her mind lost the fight. She wrapped her arms around him and he pulled her closer until she could feel the hardness between his legs. His hand slid under her shirt and across her bare skin.

Panic engulfed Asta as Jorund's hand skimmed over her scarred back. She knew the minute he felt them for his kiss softened. She pushed away from him and stepped back. He stood there, his mind half dazed from the passion he felt for her and half angered at what someone had done to her.

"Don't ask me about it, I don't want to lie to you." She tucked her shirt into her trousers. "I think I should go now. Phaedra is probably looking for me." She turned to leave when one of Jorund's men opened the door. He looked from Asta to Jorund, his face turning red with the realization of what had taken place.

"Sorry, sir. Wanted to let you know we will be ready to sail at sunrise."

"Thank you, Thork."

When the man was gone she looked back to Jorund. "Are you going somewhere?"

"I have offered the use of my ship for transport. As he said, we leave at sunrise." Jorund took a few steps toward her. "Why do you ask? Will you miss me while I am gone?" A smile played across his lips.

What an arrogant fool.

"Only as much as one would miss a wet shoe!"

Asta could still hear his booming laughter, even as she made her way off of the ship. Not once did she notice the way his crew looked at her with their knowing smiles.

The water in the tub was now cold. The once hot water did little to ease Asta's muscles, but she would not complain, for it was exercise well needed. It had been a long time since she had practiced her fighting skills and today had been a good day to vent some of her frustrations.

After she had left Jorund's ship earlier that day, she had walked back toward the tower, meeting Phaedra on the way.

"Where is Gunnar?"

"He is making his rounds to some of the sick."

Asta was never one to avoid the obvious, and Phaedra had never spoken of Gunnar, but she could see there was something between the two.

"How is it going with you and Gunnar?"

"It is nothing serious, just someone to keep me busy," Phaedra answered, trying to avoid Asta's gaze.

"You can tell me the truth."

Phaedra stopped and turned toward Asta. "There is no room for anything permanent in our lives. We would not be safe, as you have reminded me."

"You could settle, Phaedra. It is me who brings the danger, not you."

"I would never part from you, Asta. You are the reason I am alive and well. What I do is for entertainment only. Remember that, and never speak of leaving without me again."

"Fine, anything you say," Asta agreed, but she knew deep down that one day, and soon, they would have to part for the sake of Phaedra's happiness.

With neither having anything to do, Asta decided to take Phaedra to meet Marynn.

Both were quiet as they continued around the wall and into the open field.

"What is that?" Phaedra asked, walking toward the large stone monument.

"It's a burial mound of all the villagers killed in the raid." Asta walked over and stood next to Phaedra.

"Are they buried here too?"

"Their bodies were thrown over the cliff, only their heads found." Asta glanced up at the names on the monument. She knew who Phaedra asked about.

"A part of them will always be here in the memories of the few survivors and the stories they pass on. As I told you, the laird's wife, Lucia, was never found. They think she may have been taken, but I know that to not be a fact. The monument was erected in honor of the two men. They were tortured by being forced to watch as the people were killed and the village burnt."

"How cruel."

"Come, let us move on. Enough has happened of late and I do not want to dwell in this place."

Phaedra followed Asta into the forest where they could hear the rushing waters of the small stream. A short time later they were entering the clearing. The cottage was there as it had been before, its windows open, grey plumes still rising from the chimney.

"What a cozy-looking cottage."

"I know Marynn will be excited to meet you." Asta knocked on the door, but there was no answer so she stepped inside the house. The fire was burning bright but no one was there.

"She wouldn't go far with the fire burning."

Laughter filled the air, followed by the sounds of water splashing. Asta followed Phaedra to the back of the cottage. They stopped and watched as Marynn climbed up the side of the stream, her hair wild and her dress soaked to her knees. She kept her apron tight against her to hold what was clearly fish.

Another scene flashed before Asta's eyes of a young woman with flowing red locks, her small daughter following her up from the water.

"Is that her?"

Phaedra's voice broke the image, and as fast as it came, it was gone.

"Yes, that is her." Asta watched Marynn come closer, struggling to hold her bundle.

"Asta? Is that you, child? You came just in time." The smile widened across Marynn's face.

"Marynn, I have brought someone for you to meet."

"It must be Phaedra."

"How did you know?"

"You talked of her much on your last visit." Marynn continued on into the cottage with the girls following behind.

They sat down as Marynn emptied her load onto a large wooden block. Four large fish lay there, their gills still moving, the freshest still flopping around. Marynn picked up a small axe and removed its head first before finishing with the others. She gutted and cleaned them, setting each one aside when finished.

"You are quieter than I thought you would be, Phaedra. Is there something amiss?"

Phaedra jumped slightly when Marynn spoke her name.

"No, yes, well…it's just that…"

"Come now, tell me what's on your mind."

Asta looked at Phaedra, smiling, arching one eyebrow, as if she too was waiting for an answer.

Phaedra looked back to Marynn who was still working on the fish.

"You are blind but catch fish better than any man I have ever known. How is that possible?"

Marynn burst out laughing. "Men look for a spot to fish hoping they will get a catch. I stand in the water and wait for the fish to come to me."

"But you can't see them. How do you know when they are coming?"

"I listen to the water flow. It changes when a fish swims with it."

"Really?"

"Amazing!"

Asta and Phaedra both said in unison.

"I have been blind for a long time, girls. My hearing is all I have, so I have learned to use it well. Now, if you don't mind, you two can carry that cauldron to the stream for me and fill it with water. And don't try to tell me you're not hungry. Once you smell my fish and potato soup, your stomach will be singing."

Marynn was laughing as they went to the stream to fill the pot.

"She's a little crazy, don't you think?" Phaedra asked as they reached the water.

"You would be to if you had to endure what she has, though I do think she is more outspoken than crazy."

"Reminds me of someone I know." Phaedra wasn't expecting the water, so when Asta splashed it toward her it soaked her from head to waist.

Asta couldn't hold back the burst of laughter that came forth, but when she saw the look on Phaedra's face, she knew she had better defend herself. Looking around the ground, she armed herself with the biggest stick she could find and held it in front of her like a sword.

"So you want to play, do you?" Phaedra found a stick of her own and crossed it with Asta's. "Are you sure you are up for this? Your wound is still healing."

"It is but a scratch." With that said, Asta made the first move, bringing her stick down hard on Phaedra's.

Within minutes they were into a full one-on-one battle. Both women were taking the other's blows, maneuvering out of harm's way, and coming back hard again. Their concentration was so deep that neither noticed the small figure that was watching from the bushes.

The bushes gave him a great view of both the women as they expertly wielded their sticks. If they were playing he could not tell, for their faces showed great control. There was movement from the cottage as Marynn made her way toward the sound. She stopped and listened, her hand covering her mouth.

A loud crack split the air and then silence as both women looked to their broken sticks and then each other. It was Phaedra who started to laugh first, but it wasn't long before Asta joined in.

"Injury or not, you still fight like a man."

"So do you."

"I'm not the one recovering from an encounter with death."

"If you girls are finished playing, I could use that water now." Marynn was standing at the back of the cottage, the axe still held tight in her hand.

"We are coming." Asta crouched down, holding the large pot on one side with Phaedra on the other. It slowly filled with water and they watched as Marynn went back into the cottage.

"You have to admit she looked a little crazy just then."

"I will say she did."

Both women laughed all the way back to the cottage.

Now, rising out of her bath, Asta laughed aloud as she recalled the day's events and finished drying herself. Dressing in a long white shirt, she sat on the bed and combed her hair, which was the one luxury she had allowed herself over the years.

The ivory and silver comb she used had once belonged to her mother. There were a few prongs missing, but it still worked well. It was one of the two things she had been able to keep secret throughout the years. The other was the medallion.

Her mother had left it with her when she hid her in the forest.

A knock on the door interrupted her thoughts. She stood from the bed, wrapped one of the blankets around her, and walked to the window, placing the comb on the table.

"You may come in."

Two young boys entered the room. She sat in the chair, the light breeze from the window blowing through her damp hair, and waited while they took the water away and closed the door behind them.

She sat quietly thinking about all that she had learned here. She would leave soon, which brought another question to mind. How would she say good-bye to Phaedra without her following?

It was late into the night when she left the chair and crawled into bed.

He was chilled to the bone, weary from hours of riding, and this gloomy, rainy day was taking a toll on his temper. He looked out toward the ocean, its waves pounding ferociously on the cliffs below. Lightning irradiated the sky, revealing a ship in the distance, its white sails glowing against the dark of the storm. When the sky lit up again the ship was almost out of sight.

A piercing scream echoed through the mist.

He looked ahead to see the men riding hard along the path and disappearing around the bend in the forest. He could see the smoke, even smell it, as he kicked his horse into a run. When he entered the village he was sick from the sight before him. The smoke from the burning houses stung his eyes and lungs, but he stood there in shock as he looked around at the men, women, and children who had been slaughtered.

Something was shining at his feet. He reached down to pick it up. It was a dagger, and on its handle was…

Jorund sat up in bed, his heart pounding wildly. His hand was trembling as he wiped the sweat from his face. All those dead bodies, the fires, the smoke, everything came rushing back. Anger swept through him. It had been years since he had dreamed of that day, years since he had felt the pain of losing what he loved so much.

He crawled from the bed and left the room, pulling his trousers on as he went. He made his way to where Asta slept, raised his hand to knock, and paused. It was late and he was sure she was asleep. He entered the room without making a noise. The cot at the end of the bed was empty. He scanned the room, but Phaedra was nowhere to be seen. From the information he had gathered from his men, she spent some of the night watching over his village and the rest in the company of Gunnar.

The moonlight spilled across the bed, outlining Asta's sleeping form. He quietly made his way toward her, stopping at the edge of the bed. She was curled up with one hand under her pillow, the other under her chin. The anger he had felt so intensely started to fade. With his anger gone, sleep started to beckon to him. It was a few hours until sunrise and he had a big day ahead of him. He reached for the blanket she had kicked to the floor and, stifling a yawn, began to cover her.

Asta was awake but didn't open her eyes when she heard someone enter the room. She knew it wasn't Phaedra, for she had gone to watch the village as she so often did and wouldn't return until morning. Her grip tightened on the knife under her pillow and she tried to keep her breathing steady as the stranger moved to the edge of the bed. Could this be the same person who started the fire?

The movement she felt on her legs spurred her into motion. With the speed of an expert, she rose up, placing her blade against the attacker's throat and her other hand at the back of his neck. He raised his head, the moon illuminating his face.

Her heart sank.

"What are you doing in here?" Though she was still shaking with fear inside, Asta asked the question in a soft, calm voice.

"What are you doing with a knife?" Jorund's voice was just above a whisper, but she could still hear his aggravation.

"Why do you always answer a question with a question?" she asked, glaring coldly at him. She didn't care if he was mad. He shouldn't be sneaking around in the dark scaring people.

"I was checking on you and the blanket was kicked off the bed. I was covering you up."

Asta glanced down to see his hand still gripping the thin material. She looked back to his face, their eyes locking.

"Can you remove the blade from my throat now?"

She let out a light gasp and dropped her hands to her sides, but he didn't move. It was then that Asta realized how close they were. She felt the soft caress of his breath across her face as he spoke.

"It's your turn to answer. What are you doing with a knife?" He reached out to take it from her and she let him have it, never breaking eye contact.

"It's for protection." A slight smile hovered on her lips. "You never know when someone may enter your room in the middle of the night." She heard the clatter of the knife as it hit the floor. Her heart began beating wildly, her breath coming in short puffs.

"You should not be in this room, Jorund."

"You should not be in my bed, Asta."

It was still dark outside but sunrise was rapidly approaching. Jorund made his way out of the tower and into the village. This was the last thing he wanted to do. He would rather be in the bed with Asta's warm body next to his. The image of her sleeping form wrapped in nothing but the cover was burned into his mind. The past night had proved to be something he would enjoy repeating night after night with her.

He took a deep breath of the morning air to clear his head. He wanted her, forever. He would make her his wife, but there were questions he needed answers to first, and since she wasn't willing to give them, he would find out himself.

Jorund reached his destination and knocked heavily on the door. It took a moment before he heard movement inside, then the door opened.

"Jorund?" Gunnar stood there, hair tousled, still pulling on his clothes. "Is something wrong?" He looked behind him before waving Jorund in, then he closed the door and walked to the fire to stir the dying embers.

Jorund sat at the table and waited to speak until Gunnar had joined him.

"I want you to ride out to the surrounding lands and see if anyone might know about our two guests."

Gunnar's eyes widened. He looked away and then back to Jorund. "Has something happened?"

Jorund thought on how to phrase his words without giving away the past night's events. "Nothing bad has happened. My patience has run out and I want answers, now. I will leave it at that." Jorund rose and moved to leave. "I will depart soon and, if all goes well, will return on the seventh day. I wish for you to do the same. Gather what information you can and meet me back here."

"You are sure nothing's wrong?"

"We will figure that out when you return. The guards are on extra patrol and I have been given use of more than a dozen men from the visiting lords. All should be well until my return."

"I will ready my things."

"Then I will see you on the beach shortly."

Jorund left Gunnar's house and headed toward the beach to make sure the men were ready for their departure.

The dream he had last night was still fresh in his mind, and though he couldn't put his finger on it, there was something there that bothered him. He only hoped that when Gunnar returned it was with good news.

Gunnar watched the door close then turned his sight to the woman coming from behind the curtain that separated the room.

"I think it's time you tell me everything." He watched her hips sway back and forth as she moved toward him.

"I have already told you my story. As to why we are here, that is Asta's story and hers to tell." Phaedra sat across his lap and wrapped her arms around his neck, but the affection was not returned.

"I am leaving today to find information about you. What happens when I return?"

"Whatever you want to happen, will."

"What kind of life will we have together if you keep secrets?"

The smile faded from her lips. She started to rise, but he placed his hands on her hips to stop her.

"I don't want anything to come between us. Tell me, Phaedra, please."

The tears began to gather in her eyes but she forced them back. "I can't. I'm sorry, Gunnar. Please understand."

"So this is how it will be." He loosened his hold on her.

Walking to the door she paused at the threshold but did not turn around. "She saved my life and I owe her beyond what

I could ever give back. I hope that one day she will be brave enough to tell her story, but until then, well, you will just have to trust me when I say we mean no disrespect by being silent. For Asta, silence is the only safety she has left."

Gunnar was left alone staring at the closed door. After a few minutes he moved around the house gathering supplies before heading for the beach. There were questions he needed answers to himself. The sooner he left, the sooner he would have them.

Asta opened her eyes to an empty bed. The sun was beginning to show over the horizon, its light reaching through the window, outlining Phaedra's sleeping form. Asta climbed out of bed, crossing the room as quietly as possible, and ducked behind the screen to dress. Her arms and legs were sore from the night's activity, only adding to the discomfort from the past day's strenuous exercise. But her spirits were high, her skin still tingling, as the image of Jorund making love to her played over again through her head.

Jorund had kissed her, fully and passionately, as she kneeled on the bed. Warning bells rang through her head, but when he circled his arms around her, pulling her closer, the thrumming of her body drowned out the logical thinking of her brain. Only when his hands skimmed over her back did her body tense, but the soothing words he whispered to her soon had her pulling him closer. He stripped her of her clothes, laid her down on the bed then removed his own and joined her. It was as they were made one that Jorund ceased his movements.

And she knew why.

Never had she joined with another like this. The sharp pain brought tears to her eyes, but was nothing compared to the shock in his. As quickly as it came the look was gone and he was again whispering soothing words to her as he kissed the wetness from her cheeks.

Asta shook the images from her head, finished dressing, and left the room, closing the door on Phaedra's light breathing. All was quiet as she made her way down the stairs and across the great hall. The tower was empty with the exception of the young woman who was cleaning the dirty cook area.

"Where is everyone?"

"Down at the boats seeing the men off."

Asta had almost forgotten that Jorund was leaving today. She was upset over his quick departure, but she could not let her heart dictate her actions. Last night was as much her fault as it was his and she knew it could not happen again. Apparently he felt the same as he was leaving with no word to her. What did she think would happen? There was no admittance of love or promises of a life together so she could not expect him to be waiting for her today.

With her good mood retreating, she declined the offer to sit and eat; instead opting for a chunk of bread, then left the girl to her chores. She stepped out of the tower, her hair glowing amber in the rising sun, and continued out the tower gates into the village. The merchants were busy setting up their booths for the selling or trading of their many wares. This, she decided, would be a good day to see what was on display.

The first booth she stopped at was run by a small woman who was tottering on her feet thanks to her protruding belly.

"Good morning to you, miss," the woman said as she arranged the different urns and jars she had on display.

Asta nodded and continued on. This was so familiar to her, the scents of spices, aroma of freshly cooked meats, many colors of beautiful fabrics. She had frequented many bazaars in her travels and this she would call the same. She was halfway through the stands when something caught her eye. Up ahead was a jeweler's stand. Behind him hung the most exquisite gemstone necklace she had ever seen.

"What is it?" she asked, coming up to the front of the small shop.

A tall, burly man with short blond hair turned from what he was doing to see who was talking to him. He followed Asta's gaze to the wall behind him and the glass-enclosed necklace that hung there.

"That is the Jord necklace."

"The Jord necklace?"

"Yes, so it was named by the ruler who bought it for his daughter. They say she is so beautiful that she is the reincarnation of the earth goddess herself. She wears the real necklace."

"What is it made of?"

"The deep blue gem in the middle is sapphire. The greenish-blue gems surrounding it are aquamarine mined from Madagascar. All are held together by the gold that forms the rope it hangs from."

It was larger than the palm of her hand, but its unique look made it bigger than the world.

"I have never seen anything so stunning."

"I hope not. It is one of a kind. My brother designs the jewelry and I make it."

"Why display it if it is not real?"

"My brother thought that it was of such great work that it would attract people to our shop."

"And so it has, for here I am asking about it. It is great work."

"I am Bruno," he said as he held his hand out to her, "and my brother's name is Ivan. We thank you for the compliment."

"I am Asta," she replied, shaking his hand. "Where do you come from?"

"Everywhere. My mother was a traveler, though I do know she belonged to a Germanic tribe along the Danube River. She migrated down the Rhine River after we were born and we have travelled since, never staying in one place too long."

"And your mother still travels with you?" Asta was so engrossed with the many odd pieces of jewelry scattered about the shelves that she missed the disheartened look in Bruno's eyes.

"Sadly, no, she was killed in a raid a few years back."

Asta quickly looked at Bruno, but he had turned his back to her and continued working.

"I am sorry to hear that."

"Do not be. She was very ill and it was her time to go."

Asta leaned slightly over the counter to see the piece he was working on. He held it up so that she could inspect his work. The suns ray's shone down upon the gold filigree chain and through the gem it carried, entrancing her with its brilliant yellows, reds, and greens.

"What is that called?"

"It is an opal."

"It's beautiful."

"Thank you. This I designed myself."

"Where did you find such a stone?"

"We came across a vendor on our travels through India. He had only three gems like this. My brother did not want them, but I purchased them anyway. Two of my designs have already sold for quite a good price." He set the necklace across the counter for her to see. "My finished work."

The gem was held in a gold encasement that covered the back but kept the front open. It had six small gold claws that curved up and around the opal to hold it securely. The gold chain it hung from was actually three chains braided together and connected at the ends with a loop on one side and a clasp on the other.

"So, are you interested?"

Asta's smile turned to a crooked grin. "As much as I would love to own such a magnificent piece of work, I must decline and say good day to you, for I am sure you have work to do."

"It was a pleasure to meet you, Asta. I am sure I will see you around."

She left Bruno watching her with curiosity as she walked off.

Asta entered the clearing and walked to the small cottage. The windows were open, the fire burning, but there was no answer to her knocking.

"Marynn?" She knocked again and opened the door.

There was no one there so she entered to wait. Immediately she noticed two swords in their leather-bound scabbards leaning against the table.

She sat in a chair lifting a sword into her lap, untied the straps, and grasped the iron handle. She pulled the blade free, noticing there was no design to identify who it belonged to. It had been sharpened and shined so someone had taken great care of it. She put the scabbard down and stood raising the sword to test its weight. The blade was wide and heavy, but years of training had toned her arms to handle such weight.

"I found them as I was leaving this morning. They were outside my door." Marynn entered the house with a few potatoes, a slab of beef, and a bag of greens she put onto the large wooden block. She was followed by Ian whose arms were laden with wheat, beets, and a bundle of brown sticks that had a sweet and spicy smell.

"Cinnamon, it has been a long time since I have smelled that." Asta set the sword on the table and went to help Marynn place her items on the shelf while Ian went to fetch some water.

"So you have seen this spice before? You must have travelled far."

"I have been as far as the Caspian Sea." Asta finished putting up the items and turned back to the table. She knew Marynn was waiting for answers that Asta was not yet ready to give.

"So who do they belong to?" Asta picked the sword up and swung it in small circles hoping Marynn would not press her to talk of her past.

"I don't know. They were just there." Marynn laid the slab of beef out flat and, using her small dagger, began cutting pieces from it.

"There is no marking of any kind on the hilt, and the blade has been newly sharpened and shined, though the sword looks to be fairly old." Asta put this sword down and picked up the other. Untying it, she pulled it free of its scabbard and examined it. "They are almost identical, though this one feels lighter and is slightly smaller."

"It may be that someone had seen you and Phaedra out by the river a few days past and thought you could use the real thing."

Asta turned to look at Marynn, but she just continued to slice the beef. She did have great hearing if she knew what they had been up to. Ian came in struggling with the pot of water.

"I think I will keep them until someone comes to claim them." Asta placed the sword next to the other on the table then helped Ian carry the pot to the fire. They lifted it to the hook that was supported by the bar in the hearth and stepped back.

"That will do, Ian." Marynn wiped her hands on her apron and gave Ian a tight hug. "You come back at dusk for supper and I will send some with you for your papa, all right?"

Ian nodded vigorously as he ran out the door, but not before Asta saw the look on his face as he ran past the swords. It was a look of triumph and glee, and the more she thought of it the more sense it made.

There weren't many who came to see Marynn, but Ian seemed to be her main visitor. He was also the blacksmith's son, which would give him access to tools. With a blacksmith for a father, Asta was sure Ian had learned a thing or two about the trade, which included the making of swords.

Asta sat at the table and turned her attention back to Marynn. "So you knew what we were up to?"

"As I have told you before, I have excellent hearing. I know that sound, whether it be swords or sticks. You and Phaedra were not playing that day, you were battling."

"No, we were playing around."

"Do not try to dissuade me, Asta. I know the difference between play and real. You may have been playing, but you take it as training nonetheless. With the distance you have travelled I can only assume you have had to defend yourself many times." Marynn finished putting the cut meat into the pot before wiping her hands on her apron and sitting in the chair opposite Asta.

"I will not ask you to tell me, only to trust me. I want you to know that what is said or done here will never be repeated to anyone." There was a long silence before Marynn went back to her table and continued preparing her food.

Asta took a deep breath and, keeping her gaze on the forest outside the window, began to tell Marynn what she wanted to hear.

"I don't remember much about my childhood," she lied. Not everything needed to be told. "From the time I can remember I was raised with my cousin. He was the only child from my father's sister, who had died during childbirth. He had no father so his uncle, my father, raised him. It wasn't a happy time, for my mother had died also. I was trained by my father, along with my cousin, to fight and be a warrior. My cousin was not happy with this and took every chance he could get to torture me without my father knowing." On and on the story went. Asta told Marynn of the long journeys they endured and the battles they fought, though she omitted the worst, and best of all the grand cities they had travelled to.

Throughout the day Asta told Marynn of her adventures while she helped cook. Before they knew it, Ian was back at the house followed by Phaedra.

"I knew I could find you here." Phaedra nudged Asta in the side before being ushered into a chair by Marynn.

"You two are just in time." Marynn took some dishes from her shelf and within minutes she had three steaming bowls of stew, a platter of fresh sliced bread, and mugs of ale spread out before them.

"Eat up and I will make you some to take." Marynn ruffled Ian's hair then went to make his food to take.

"I thought you would have been there to see Jorund off, Asta." Phaedra passed the slices of bread, first to Ian then to Asta, before taking some herself.

Asta was not eating. She was staring at Phaedra in astonishment, her heart beating faster than the blowing wind. Did Phaedra know of last night? Did she see Jorund leave the room?

"Why would I have been there?"

"It is customary to see the leader of the village off when he embarks on a journey. You were the one to say we should respect the customs of others," Phaedra pointed out in between bites.

"I didn't know it was." Asta took a bite of her stew relieved that her night was still unknown. "Besides, he was already on the ship when I woke. I'm sure he set sail shortly after."

"No, he didn't. It was midday when he set sail. I looked for you but you were gone."

A cold numbness came over Asta.

Jorund was trying to avoid her. He probably didn't want to explain to her that last night was a mistake. Well, she was glad she didn't see him off, she didn't need his explanations. All those whispered words meant nothing, were only said to get her in the bed with him. She understood just fine. She pushed her food away from her.

"Asta, are you well? You look awfully pale." Phaedra rose from the table and walked around to Asta, placing her hand on her head. "You're not hot."

Asta pushed Phaedra's hand away. "I'm fine, just not hungry."

"You need some fresh air. You've been in this house with me all day." Marynn set a small pot on the table next to Ian and with it a loaf of cloth-wrapped bread. "This is for your father, and there should be extra for on the morrow." She took his empty bowl and went to the fire to fill it back up. "While you are out there you could show Phaedra the gifts from your secret admirer."

"What secret admirer?" Phaedra asked.

Asta had already gone to retrieve the swords from under Marynn's bed. Earlier in the day she had asked to keep them there and Marynn had agreed. She slid the bundle from under the bed and unwrapped the blanket she had set them in.

Phaedra followed Asta to the back of the cottage and into the open area by the stream. This is where Asta handed Phaedra the smallest sword.

"They are the same, though yours is slightly smaller and lighter than mine."

Phaedra stood there holding the sword in bewilderment.

"It is beautiful, is it not?" Asta was now standing on the far side of the clearing swinging her sword so her body could get used to the weight of it.

"Who gave these to you?" Phaedra untied the straps and slid the sword from its scabbard.

"They were left at Marynn's door. I have a feeling they were made for us."

"There was nothing to explain where they came from or who left them?"

"Nothing."

"There are no markings." Phaedra ran her fingers over the soft metal of the hilt then she swung the sword a few times to test its weight. "It may be a trap."

"I don't think so." Asta came to stand in front of Phaedra. "I have a notion that a young boy has been watching us, may even admire us so much that he thought to give us a gift."

"Who, Ian?"

"Why not? His father is a blacksmith."

Phaedra lifted her sword to eye level. "Look at this sword, Asta. It is perfect. If it is as strong as it looks, then it had to have been made by an expert, not a young boy."

Asta raised her sword to cross Phaedra's. "I believe it is as strong as it looks, so if you are up to it, we can test it. I'm sure Ian would love the show considering he has been watching us since we came back here."

Phaedra turned her head and spotted Ian peeking around the corner.

"He may just be curious." She turned back to Asta. "But I will gladly fulfill his curiosity."

The sun was almost completely set as Marynn made her way toward the stream. She could no longer hear the clanking of steel but instead followed laughter. Both girls were kneeling down at the edge of the stream cleaning the small scratches on their arms that had been caused from their swordplay.

"How is your side feeling?" Phaedra finished washing away the blood and drying her arms on her cloak.

"It is a bit sore, but it was worth it." Asta stood shaking the water from her arms. "It won't feel so tight once the scabbing peels away."

"I'm glad you stopped when you did. I fear I would have to explain why you were in so much pain after visiting me." Marynn was standing a few feet away from them, a huge grin on her face. "Ian has already left, so unless you don't mind if someone sees you, I suggest you put up the swords and head back to the tower before they send a search party."

"We were just finishing. It's getting too dark to see anyhow." Asta picked up Phaedra's scabbard and gave it to her before retrieving hers from the ground.

They followed Marynn into the cottage. Asta wrapped the swords in the blanket, slid them under the bed, then wished Marynn a good night.

"I will be waiting for your return on the morrow."

They had left the house and were in the forest when Phaedra spoke to Asta.

"Has Marynn ever mentioned her past to you?"

"She has only told me of the village's past, never anything specifically to do with her. Why?"

"I was wondering how she came to have the scars on her face."

"So you have seen them too?" Asta slowed her steps so that they walked side by side. "At first I thought they were deep wrinkles."

"I've seen her face in the rays of the fading sun. They are scars. That may be the reason she never goes into the village."

"That could be. I have never seen her go into the village but stand by the outer gate while Ian and others bring her what she needs."

They came out of the forest, crossed the open field, and walked around the wall into the village.

"I was hoping that at first light you could accompany me to the stones. I want to see them while Jorund is not here to follow me. Do you think you could put Gunnar off for a bit?"

"That should be no problem. He left this day and will not return for a few moons."

"I didn't know he was travelling with Jorund."

"He is not, but he did go to do business for him."

Asta noticed how Phaedra tensed at the mention of Gunnar, but she let it go assuming they were having problems.

"Good, then we can leave at sunrise and return by late noon to visit with Marynn."

They stood at the tower gates waiting for the guards to permit them entrance. Once the gates began to open, Phaedra made her farewells.

"I told Lydia I would check on her. She is one of Gunnar's patients and is due with child at any moment. She is very nervous with Gunnar's absence." Phaedra hugged Asta and confirmed she would be waiting at the gates in the morning, then she left.

Asta watched as Phaedra disappeared into the crowd of villagers that were slowly dispersing to their homes for the night. She walked through the gates, the only light being from the torches scattered about the yard and hanging by the entrance to the tower.

Once inside, she made her way to the cookery using the light cast by the glow of the fire pit. The sting of her arms was only slight, but the cuts needed to be cleaned again. There was a young girl sitting by the large fire in the hearth. When she noticed Asta she sprang up out of the chair.

"Dania said you may want a bath. I will fetch some of the boys and have them carry up some water for you."

Asta had not expected to take a bath, only to have a bucket of water to cleanse with. "Thank you. I would love a bath. What is your name?"

"Reah."

"I am Asta, though I'm sure you knew that." She reached out to take the girl's hand but Reah didn't move. She was too engrossed with the small cuts across Asta's arm.

Asta tucked her arm back under her cloak.

"Do you know where Dania may be?"

"She is out helping some of the women with their preparations for the festival. She should return soon."

"Thank you again for the bath, Reah."

Asta left the cookery, crossed the hall, and taking a torch from the wall, she made her way up the stairs. The water tub wasn't the first thing she saw when she entered the room. It was the small wooden box wrapped in a blue ribbon that sat upon her bed. She lit the candles in the stand, placed the torch in the wall hanger outside the door, then went to her bed and picked up the box. Included with the box was a folded piece of parchment with the simple initial J written on it.

Her heart fluttered and her hands shook as she slid the ribbon from the box. When she opened it she was not prepared for the brilliance of its contents. A long chain with hundreds of interlocking gold rings sat inside attached to a large opal. She lifted the necklace from the box and watched as the candlelight shone on it, causing magnificent oranges and reds to dance inside the gem.

A sudden thought came to mind.

She had talked to Bruno earlier in the day and he had said there were three opals, two of which had been sold, and the third he had finished today. A shiver of excitement crept up her spine.

Had Jorund purchased the necklace before they had spent the night together? She had thought the worst of him, thinking he was telling lies to get her in his bed. Had he been waiting for her to come to him and say good-bye? Had he watched the beach as he sailed away hoping to get a glimpse of her?

It was for the best that she had not been there.

She dropped the necklace back into the box and closed the lid. She could never stay here, the danger was too great, and she shouldn't lead Jorund on by accepting his gift. It was best if she stayed clear of him once he returned. She didn't want him to get his heart involved in something that could never be. One broken heart would be enough and hers was breaking with every day that passed, for she knew it wouldn't be long before she was well enough to leave. Regardless of how she tried to deny it, her heart was already full of love for him.

Asta was brought out of her reverie by the sound of soft knocking at the door. She pushed the box under her pillow and dropped the ribbon in the basket next to the bed.

"Come in."

Two boys carried in steaming pots of hot water followed by four more carrying the same. They poured their loads into the iron tub and left. A moment later Dania entered with a tray full of scented oils and soaps. She placed them, along with a stack of clothes, on the table that had been set next to the tub then turned to Asta.

"Are you well, dear? Reah has told me your arms had been scratched."

"I was helping Marynn gather sticks for her fire." Asta blurted out the first thing thought that came to mind.

"Let me see. I may have something to soothe the pain."

"There's really no pain."

"There will be once the water gets on it." Dania helped Asta out of her cloak then examined her arms. She returned to the tray and pulled up a single bottle. "Once you are done with your bath, apply this lightly across the cuts. It will soothe them and help them to heal faster." Dania placed the bottle on the table. "Everything else is scented. I will leave you to your bath now. The boys will retrieve the tub later."

"Good night, Dania, and thank you."

Dania smiled at Asta and departed, closing the door behind her.

Asta finished undressing and climbed slowly into the tub. Her side was hurting, but the heat of the water helped ease the pain and her aching muscles. She took one of the towels from the table and, folding it, placed it on the edge of the tub behind her head. Then she lay back and let the water do its work.

It wasn't until her arms slid under the water that she realized she had dozed off. The pain wasn't bad, but the sting of the raw cuts woke her out of her sleepy haze.

She pulled the first vial off the tray and lifted its wax lid, but she quickly covered the strong-smelling liquid and put it back. The next vial smelled of roses. She inhaled the soft scent then put it back, reaching for the next. None were to her liking so she opted for the ball of soap.

This, she thought as she lathered the soap, was the best decision. Its lavender scent wafted up, surrounding her with its sweet euphoria. She scrubbed her hair then worked the soap over the rest of her body, careful not to be hard on her wounds.

Once she was done she rinsed the soap off with the now tepid water. She stepped from the tub and began drying herself. Wrapping the large cloth around her, she reached for the bottle Dania had pointed out and sat by the window to apply it to her arms. After a while she dressed and returned to the chair, brushing her hair out with her ivory comb.

It wasn't long before the boys came to retrieve the tub, and she was once again left alone, her thoughts going to Jorund and the necklace. With a heavy heart she made the decision to give it back when he returned, but in the meantime it wouldn't hurt to try it on. She took the box from under her pillow and lifted the necklace from it. Then, clasping it around her neck, she lay down on the bed enjoying the feel of the cold stone as it rested against her chest.

Asta was only slightly awakened by Phaedra's loud whispers, but she bolted upright when the bed was violently shaken.

"Get up. The sun will rise soon and we need to get going." Phaedra was standing next to her, a single candle burning in one hand and the other still shaking the bed.

"I'm awake. You can stop now."

"Good. I'm going to get a few supplies from the cookery. Get dressed and meet me down there." Phaedra lit the candle next to Asta's bed and left the room.

Asta rolled from the bed, her hand quickly going to the weight at her neck. She unclasped the necklace, placed it back in its box, and slid it under her pillow. She dressed in her usual attire of trousers and loose shirt, tied her hair back, then went to the wall at the side of the bed and removed the loose brick. This is where she had hidden the medallion the first night she had come back with Phaedra. When she was sure the brick was placed back in its secure spot, she grabbed her cloak, tucking the medallion safely in the pocket, and went to find Phaedra.

She was outside by the stables but she was not alone. Ian was there along with three horses.

"Well, I didn't know we would have company. What a surprise."

"I didn't want Dania to be worried when we couldn't be found, so I told her we wanted to see the land. She offered the horses and I volunteered Ian as our guide."

"You asked for him to be here?"

"Dania was insisting we take someone with us. He was the safest person I could think of to accompany us. I have explained to him what we are doing and he has vowed to keep silent, so to speak. He is going to watch the horses when we get to the edge of the forest." Phaedra handed Asta's sword to her.

"When did you get these?"

"I didn't, Ian did."

"So Marynn knows where we are going too?"

"No. He said she was gone to pick her herbs and spices so he just took them and left," Phaedra said, mounting her horse. "Come on. Let's get going."

The sun was barely rising when they reached the edge of the forest. They dismounted and entered the forest, leaving Ian behind to watch the horses as planned. It wasn't much later that they reached a small hill. On the other side was the cave they had stayed in. The first time Asta made this climb she had been certain it was a mountain. The pain was unbearable, and as much as she had struggled to make it on her own, she was thankful Jorund had picked her up and carried her.

"Are you coming or are you going to stand there and day-dream?" Phaedra hollered from the top of the hill.

Asta started to climb and within minutes was at the top descending down the other side. Instead of moving toward the cave as they had the first time, they went to the left, following the forest. They walked for some time until the forest ended and opened into a large field.

There it stood. The stone circle.

Memories flooded Astas mind of a moonlit night spent with her mother surrounded by large stone giants. She pulled the medallion from her cloak.

"This is it. The last gem on the medallion is this spot here."

"Are you sure?"

"Yes." Asta walked to the stones in a trance as if the stones themselves were pulling her. Phaedra followed behind as Asta touched each stone, tracing the etched circles with her fingertips.

"So now what?" Phaedra watched as Asta walked to the flat stone in the middle of the circle.

"I'm not sure. This is where the map ends."

Phaedra walked around the circle looking for anything that would tell her what they were to do. That's when she noticed something familiar.

"Asta, look."

Asta made her way to where Phaedra stood on the far side of the circle.

"What is it?" She looked to where Phaedra pointed. The stone was etched with seven small circles and one larger circle.

"It looks like your medallion."

Asta placed her medallion next to the bigger circle. The gems matched perfectly to the etching on the stone. "They are the same size and exact space away from each other."

"And look at that." Phaedra pointed farther up the stone. The circle above was also the same size as the medallion, only this one had seven small knots where the medallion had holes. "Could there be a missing piece?"

Asta was quiet as she examined the second circle. Never in her years of studying the medallion did it occur to her there could be a second piece. But as she stood there looking at it, she knew it was the truth. Why then would her mother leave her with one and not the other? She looked closely at the medallion. For the first time she could see where another piece would fit and lock into place.

"The second piece must tell exactly where we need to be."

"We don't have the second piece."

"And I have no idea who would have it." Asta slipped the medallion back into her cloak. The sounds of horses' hoofs echoed through the forest.

"Someone's coming. No one knows we're here except Ian."

"That's not him. It sounds like four riders. Quick, hide behind one of the stones." Asta crouched down, tucking her cloak close around her while Phaedra did the same at the stone next to her.

Asta could see the shadows of the four riders as they came closer to the circle.

"I see no evidence of a fire."

"They may have not come this far. The other circles had old fire pits and crushed ground where they slept."

"Come. We have a few days' ride ahead of us. He waits for word of our findings."

"And his wrath when we tell him we have no leads."

Asta and Phaedra stayed quietly crouched down until the sounds of the horses faded to nothing. When they were sure they were alone, they stood and started back toward Ian and the horses.

"So we know for sure they are looking for us. It won't be long before they know we have been in the village." Asta didn't want to think what that would mean for the people she had come to care for in such a short time.

"They have no leads. That is what they said. He will not think to look for us there."

"But they have found evidence at the other stone circles. He will know we are in the vicinity."

Neither spoke the rest of the way, for they knew what the other was thinking. They reached Ian as the sun was passing overhead.

"We have made good time."

"We should see Marynn upon our return. We told her we would visit, and it would seem strange if we stayed locked away now. Nobody should suspect anything is wrong." Asta knew that people were already curious about them.

Asta and Phaedra gave each other a knowing look. They mounted their horses, Asta following behind, every so often looking back over her shoulder to be sure they were still alone.

The next few days were spent at Marynn's with Asta and Phaedra practicing with their swords. They hadn't seen much of Dania, for she was busy with preparations for the festival that was to begin on the morrow. Ian was a permanent fixture in their daily exercise, which only helped confirm the fact that he was the one who gave them their gifts.

But even though Asta's days kept her busy, her nights were haunted with dreams of Jorund and his warm kisses. Every night she slept with the necklace as it was the only thing that helped her sleep. And that brought another question to her mind. Why didn't Bruno tell her that Jorund had purchased the necklace?

Early one morning, as Phaedra was helping to deliver the baby of one of Gunnar's patients, Asta decided to talk with Bruno. She made her way to the shop but he was not there. Instead a small man of medium height was behind the counter.

"Excuse me, I'm looking for Bruno?"

The small man turned around, eyeing Asta suspiciously. "And you are?"

"My name is Asta. You must be Ivan."

"Asta. I have heard of you. You are the woman the laird found in the forest." He stopped what he was doing and came closer to Asta. "You are a beauty. Bruno has told me you admire our work."

"Oh yes, especially the Jord necklace."

"So you did not like the necklace you were given?"

How did he know of the necklace Jorund had given her? It seemed that everyone talked of what was happening, or not happening, between her and Jorund. Did they know of the night they spent together too? Bright red crept up Asta's neck.

"Don't get flushed. My brother told me that Jorund had purchased the necklace the day before you were admiring our work. I just assumed it was for you."

"You are right, and I like it just fine. As a matter of fact, it is a very beautiful piece of work." Asta looked around to be sure no one was listening to their conversation.

"My brother is out at the arena. He has entered the games and is practicing for the tournament."

"Thank you, Ivan." She left him to his work and made her way to the arena. She had her answer about the necklace but found she still wanted to talk to Bruno.

She found him in combat with a large man from one of the islands. Their swords clashed loudly as each man, sweating from the exertions of the fight, tried his best to knock the sword from his opponent's hands. Minutes later, that's what happened as Bruno swung hard and the other man's sword went flying into the air. The game was called and Bruno came to where Asta had sat on the benches to watch.

"What brings you to the arena, Asta?" Bruno sat next to her, wiping his face with his shirt.

"I stopped by to see you at the shop. Instead I met your brother."

"You stopped to see me? I am flattered."

"Actually, I was wondering why you didn't tell me that Jorund was the one who had bought one of your opals."

"And ruin the surprise for you?"

"You knew it was for me? Who else knew?"

"Everyone who saw him purchase it. These people are not without brains. They can see how he looks at you and you at him."

"That is not so."

"Then you can tell me I may have a chance with you?" Bruno looked at her with the light of hope in his eyes.

"No, I can't. And the same goes for him. I am to leave soon and it is not in my plans to be with any man."

"Perhaps you should tell this to Jorund. He has other plans for you, I am sure. It is not lust but love I see in his eyes when he looks at you. Tell me, Asta, if you were staying, would you want to be with him? The truth, please, I promise it will stay between you and me."

She hesitated a moment before answering. Though she hadn't known Bruno long she did feel as if she could speak to him without worry of him talking to others.

"Yes, I believe I would. But that is not an option, so I wish not to speak of it again."

"As you wish and I can accept that I will never be more than a friend. For this I will settle happily."

"Thank you, Bruno."

Days turned into a week and even more days passed. Asta split her time between practicing with Phaedra and cheering Bruno on at the arena fights, which Phaedra had joined her in watching. The festival was starting off great with food, games, crafts, and skits put on by the children. More people arrived every day, but still there was no word from Jorund.

It was early one morning that Dania, taking a break from her cooking, presented Asta with a beautiful green tunic lined with gold thread.

"I have never worn anything so exquisite." After Asta finished her bath, Dania helped her to dress and braided her hair. She wrapped it around the top of Asta's head and decorated it with a wreath of gold wire, strips of green silk, and small flower buds. The end result took Asta's breath away.

"There's one thing missing."

"What?"

"The necklace my son gave you before he left."

"You knew about that?"

"He told me of his intentions. You should wear it."

Asta's more realistic side told her it wouldn't be a good idea. But then, when would she ever look this good and be able to wear something that grand again? She retrieved it from her room and clasped it about her neck, then she stood in Dania's room in front of the floor-length mirror and didn't even recognize herself.

"Thank you." The two women hugged, tears trailing paths down both of their faces.

"You are the most beautiful woman in the entire village," Dania exclaimed before making her excuses and leaving.

Asta walked to Marynn's house to show Phaedra, who was helping Marynn cook, and everyone she passed looked in unbelieving awe at the beauty they saw. It was embarrassing to her for one reason. She had never owned or worn a dress of any kind. Trousers and shirts were the appropriate wear when she travelled and fought. Even Phaedra was taken aback by the new look.

"I don't know what to say. I never thought I would see you look this much like a woman."

"You don't like it?"

"I didn't say that. I think you look gorgeous."

"Then why do I feel that you don't approve?"

"Perhaps it has something to do with the weight you wear around your neck. There is no room for permanence. Those were your words, Asta. But here you are prancing around with a gift from a man that you deny."

"He is not here to see it."

"And you think that is alright? I told you people have been talking. They have seen you wear a gift from their laird. There is only one conclusion they can come to."

Asta sat in the chair and put her head in her hands. Marynn was not there to hear the conversation, for she was out with Ian collecting wood. It was a good thing too. She did not need anyone else to hear the admission she was about to give.

"I want him, Phaedra, more than I have ever wanted anyone." She looked up at her friend, tears brimming in her eyes. "I dream of him, every night. I even sleep with the necklace on so I can feel closer to him. But there's something in me that forces me to push it all away."

"Don't let him slip away. I know he can make you happy, Asta."

"But what if I tell him the truth and he turns his back on me?"

"That is a chance you take."

"No, I cannot. It would be better if I never knew. I need to stay with the plan and that is to leave." She wiped her hand across her face to rid herself of the fallen tears. "I would rather him hurt from me leaving than from feeling I betrayed him."

"You may not have told him the truth, but neither did you lie."

"I will not change my course, Phaedra. But as I have told you before, you can stay when I go."

"And I have told you to never mention leaving without me."

It was almost nightfall when Asta and Phaedra made their way back to the village. As they were walking along the path to the tower, Ian came running and out of breath. He was swinging his arms wildly and pointing toward the beach.

"What is he saying?" Asta tried to calm him, but he refused.

"I think he said the ships are returning." Phaedra grasped Ian's arms to still him. "Is that it? You see the ships?"

Ian nodded his head as wildly as his arms had been swinging. When Asta saw the confirmation, she lifted her skirts and ran for the beach, Ian and Phaedra following close behind. She stopped fast as three ships came into view, Jorund's at the head of them.

Asta reached to her neck, feeling the weight of the stone as it rested there. What was she thinking wearing it where everyone could see? She turned and ran back through the village and up to her room. She closed the door behind her then retrieved the box from the table where she had left it.

In all the years under her father she had been trained to fight, kill, and take what she could. To never be below any man unless she wanted to be controlled. Now here she was wearing a man's collar, giving herself to a lifetime of obedience. Is this what she really wanted?

She looked out the window as the ships arrived. Jorund stood at the bow of his ship and she watched to see if he would look up to her when he didn't see her on the beach. Her heartbeat increased but slowed as Jorund disembarked and made his way among the crowd before disappearing beyond the wall. He was out of her sight and not once did he glance up to see if she watched.

Asta sat in the chair, her fingers lightly stroking the opal at her neck. Was he angry with her for not seeing him off? Did he leave the necklace hoping for just that? Perhaps he would want it back and that would be okay. Hadn't she decided to give it back anyway?

It was moments later that she heard commotion coming from below. She stood and started for the door but stopped halfway as it was thrown open with great force. Jorund stood there tall and imposing, his breathing harsh, and the tick at the base of his neck beating rapidly. She watched his eyes as they traced a path over her body from head to toe and back again, lingering on her neck.

Jorund was frozen to the spot where he stood. His dreams of Asta did no justice to the flesh and blood standing before him. He had been gone longer than he had anticipated and it had been driving him crazy the longer he was away from her. When he had first set sail, he was sure she would be watching. When he didn't see her he had told himself that he didn't care and that he would move on without her. That was not going to happen. After the first few nights without her it was obvious to him that he would not live without her. Even if that meant he had to hold her as a prisoner.

But now, as he looked upon her and saw the necklace she wore, he knew she wanted the same. He looked over her body, remembering the soft feel of her. She had put on a bit of weight, which accentuated her curves, and her arms were slightly more sculpted than he remembered. She was wearing a dark green tunic that draped her body perfectly and her hand rested on the opal at her neck.

He wanted her, now more than ever. He entered the room, closing and locking the door behind him.

Jorund awoke the next morning as the sun was rising to start a new day. He pulled Asta's warm body closer to him. Upon his arrival at the tower, his mother had anticipated his intentions and told him he needed to do the right thing. Wed Asta. So last night he had coaxed a yes from her, though it had taken all of his control. It had been during their third time of lovemaking. He had started out slow, kissing and touching her, until she was wild with passion.

"Please, Jorund." She had begged him to ease her glorious pain and that is when he asked her.

"Agree to marry me, Asta."

"I cannot. Now, please, come to me."

He kissed her again, hard and deep, but still he held back.

"Say you will marry me."

"No."

He traced a path down her neck with his lips, then down farther still until his mouth rested at the peak of her firm breast. A shudder moved through her body and her hips arched as she pleaded with him to make her his.

"Marry me."

"No."

"Yes."

He circled her nipple with his tongue as small moans escaped her throat.

"Tell me yes, Asta. I promise I will make you happy."

"Please, Jorund."

"Become my wife." He moved even closer, and as her hips arched toward him, he moved back, holding himself out of her reach.

"Say yes."

"Yes. Yes, I will be your wife."

So tonight, before she could change her mind, they were to have the ceremony to make them man and wife.

Gunnar was weary from the many days of travel. He had stopped in over a dozen villages asking about the two females, but to no avail. It was this last village, set by the sea and one day's ride from his own, that he came across a barkeep that had information for him.

"You wouldn't be the only lad looking for two young girls. I have even heard one resembles a forest fairy."

"Yes, that would be them. You have seen these two?"

"No, not myself, though I would fancy a peek. It was a few days past that a large man with blond hair and a small army pulled in. They too were looking for these girls."

"Are they still here? Perhaps I could talk to him."

"As a matter of fact, yes, they are floating out a bit from the beach. Big white sails, red dragons printed on them."

Gunnar felt the color drain from his face. "Did you say dragons?"

"Sure did. Tail wrapped around an orange sun."

Gunnar bolted from the building, running as fast as he could toward the beach. He made a dead stop when the sails came into view. Images of a blood-soaked village, rising smoke, and billowing sails with a dragon and orange sun took over his mind. He quickly made his way back to his horse, mounted, and rode out of the village. He needed to get to Jorund before it was too late.

The sun was high and the day was cool, the breeze gently blowing across Asta's face. Phaedra rode next to her in silent companionship, enjoying the day as much as her. Asta intended to take this time to tell Phaedra of her plans to marry Jorund, and tonight, before the ceremony, she would tell him her story. He deserved to know before he committed himself to her.

They were riding through the front gates to join with the others who were on the hunt for the night's feast. Suddenly Asta's horse reared up, front legs pawing at the air. She slid backwards off the horse, falling on her back, curled up when the horse came down, and only opened her eyes when she heard the horse run toward the forest. She lay there a moment trying to get her breath as Phaedra ran to her side.

"Are you alright? What happened with the horse?"

Asta was about to answer when she heard another voice calling her name. It was getting closer, but the name it called was what kept her from speaking.

"Karis, are you hurt? Can you move?" Dania fell to her knees next to Asta, genuine concern in her eyes.

Asta started to stand, her eyes never leaving Dania's. "Why do you call me that?"

The color drained from Dania's face as she realized the mistake she had made. Before she could answer Jorund came running to Asta's side.

"What happened?" He pulled Asta into his arms, holding her as he ran his hands over her body. "Do you hurt anywhere?"

"I'm fine. It just knocked the breath from me, but I'm fine now."

"I think Phaedra and I should take her back to the tower and check her over. You go and get the horse."

Jorund took another look at Asta before letting her go. "I'll be back to check on you." He kissed her cheek and made for the direction the horse ran.

Asta let Dania lead her to the tower too stunned to argue. Phaedra followed quietly behind. The walk to Dania's room gave Asta time to think. There was only one way Dania could know of that name.

"Please, sit down." Dania offered a seat to Asta, but she declined, her angry glare pinned to Phaedra.

"How could you? I thought I could trust you, tell you anything?"

"What are you talking about?" Phaedra asked, her mind desperately trying to figure out this unexpected outburst.

"You told her. That is the only way she could know." Asta's body tensed.

Dania stepped in front of Phaedra to protect her from the fury she could see coming. "She didn't tell me anything."

Asta turned toward the door to leave. "It is time for me to go."

"I knew your father."

Asta's hand stopped on the door.

"Not the brute you call a father, but your real father, and your mother too."

Asta slowly turned around, hesitantly making her way back to the chair Dania had offered. "I'm listening," she said, sitting down.

Dania ushered Phaedra into the chair next to Asta and then sat opposite them. "You look just like her, you know. I knew from the first time you opened your eyes to me. That deep bluish green is rare, and only one other I know had it. Lucia."

Asta watched Dania's eyes cloud over with unshed tears as grieving memories filled their depths.

"You need to know everything from the beginning. My husband, Jarod, was once a great warrior. He was friends with one of the most ruthless Norsemen I have ever encountered. His name was Jarl. So close were they that they claimed to be lost brothers. They took no mercy on those they dubbed weaker than themselves. Death and destruction was what they left in their path, and everyone who had heard of them would cower at the mere mention of their names. When I first saw them they were travelling through Bulgar selling their slaves. I myself was a slave, owned by an evil cutthroat who ripped me from my home and killed my family." She inhaled deeply before continuing.

"Jarod bought me that day, though to this day I don't know what attracted him to me. At the time he was with another woman, though nobody knew, not even me. I stayed with him as a slave, cooking, cleaning, and doing anything he asked of me. But he didn't treat me like others treated their slaves. He was rarely around, never bothered me, and I felt almost free. He looked at me rather funny when he was around. I would catch it out of the corner of my eye. It wasn't long before I noticed he was staying around me more, and after a while he was staying with me at night where before he would not. He demanded me into his bed but never touched me, only held me while we slept.

"Then one night, as we were preparing for sleep, he told me of her. She was the sister of his so-called brother. He had ended it with her for the simple fact that he had fallen in love with me. He wanted me for his woman, forever. I accepted, of course, for I had fallen in love with him too." Tears fell from Dania's eyes even as she wiped the old ones away.

"It was bad from the start. Not our love, but the hate from others. Jarl was not happy. He accused me of changing Jarod, said I was making him weak. Then, late one night, Jarl had had too much to drink and tried to take me. They fought that night, beating each other until neither could stand. The next morning we were on a ship sailing away from everything he had ever known. We travelled here to start a new life. That's how I met your mother. She delivered both my sons."

"Does Jorund know this story?"

"He knows it all, but not who you really are. Anyway, it was years later that we learned Jarl's sister, Sorna was her name, was carrying Jarod's child when we left."

Asta's breath caught in her throat. She knew that name and the story that went with it. Phaedra recognized the name too, for her grip had tightened on Asta's arm. Neither broke eye contact with Dania as they listened intently to her story.

"We received word that she was sick and wanted Jarod to take care of her son, his son, so they planned to meet. Jarod left first, three days before me and the boys. He wanted time with his newfound son before he introduced us." Dania wiped again at the flow of tears sliding down her pale face.

"We were minutes away when we saw the first signs of smoke, but it was too late by then. Almost everyone had been slaughtered. Men, women, children, all were dead."

Asta knew what had happened, had been witness to it all. Bad dreams had plagued her for years after. She had learned to lock them up into the deepest part of her mind, but now the memories flooded back, forcing their way through the darkness into her reality.

"I was outside playing. Mother had sent me out there so Father and his friend could talk. They came in hordes, moving up from the beach. I rushed inside but was too late; they had taken over the village. Mother and I snuck out the back through the hidden door and into the forest. She hid me there and told me to be quiet." Asta was trembling from the force of the images playing through her head. Phaedra's arms encircled her for comfort, but she was still so cold. She needed to get out of there.

Asta stood and walked to the door. "I need to think. If you want to, we could talk more later." Then she left.

Phaedra stood to follow. "I will make sure she is doing fine handling all of this."

Dania stood too, and once she was alone, she grabbed her cloak and left the tower. It was time Marynn talked to Asta.

Phaedra followed Asta to the cliff behind the tower and sat down next to her on the rocky ledge.

"So now I know the whole truth. It is Torum that Jarod fathered. That is why they came, for vengeance upon the father who was responsible for the death of his mother. My family was only in the way." Everything came together now. Why the people in the village were murdered, why everyone had treated her differently as she grew up, and why Torum had hated her so much.

"What do you think would happen if they knew the same man who murdered all those people was the same man who took and raised me as his own?"

Phaedra put her arm around her friend's shoulder. "I think if they knew the entire story they would understand."

"And when they ask me why I never escaped? What do I tell them?"

"You were young, Asta. Nobody would expect you to have known what to do."

"I don't want Jorund knowing what Torum has done to me."

"He won't think you weak, Asta, no one who knew you ever did. They despise Torum for it."

"It's not only that. Don't you see it, Phaedra? I don't know how I could have missed it after all this time here."

"See what?"

"Jorund, he has the same eyes as Torum. They are brothers."

It took a moment for this to register with Phaedra. "I never realized it, but yes, they have the same eyes."

"And Dania told us that is why they came here, to meet Jarod's unknown son."

"She said that Sorna had sent the note."

"Sorna died in childbirth, which only leaves the obvious conclusion."

"Jarl sent that note to them. He must have known that she was pregnant with Jarod's baby. We need to tell them, Asta."

"Jorund will hate me for having anything to do with those people."

Phaedra watched closely as her friend stood and paced back and forth. "I thought you didn't care what anyone thought of you. It is that you truly do love him?"

"He is pleasing to the eye."

"That is not what I asked you."

"What is there to like about him? He is a stubborn, bossy man who enjoys telling me what to do." Asta stopped pacing and looked at Phaedra. "I very much love him. In fact, I am irrevocably in love with him."

Phaedra stood and hooked her arm through Asta's. "Come, let's take a walk."

They walked to the hidden path, separating long enough to follow it to the open field where the monument stood.

"I want to tell them the truth, but I can't bear to see the anguish on their faces." Asta turned to Phaedra, but she walked away. Asta followed her, keeping silent until her friend was ready to talk.

"You are my family, Asta, and you know I would never leave you, but sometimes I want more. I don't want to always be running and looking over my shoulder. I want to settle somewhere." Phaedra stopped and turned to Asta. "Gunnar has asked me to marry him and I have said yes, but the one thing that is keeping us apart is your secrets, secrets I am not willing to tell." Phaedra stood tall, head held high. "I know you do not want the burden of telling these people what you know, so if you tell me you wish to leave, I will not hesitate to follow."

Asta walked to Phaedra and put her arms around her. "Your happiness means everything to me." She stepped back to look at Phaedra. "Jorund has also asked me to be his wife and I have accepted."

Phaedra hugged Asta with great pressure. "So do you wish to tell them? I will be by your side when you do."

"Yes and as soon as possible. And they should know about Torum, for I fear we have not seen the last of him."

They made their way back to the tower giggling and talking of plans for their weddings.

"Jorund wishes to have the ceremony tonight at the feast."

"So soon?"

"He fears I will change my mind and run away." Asta's smile faltered, but Phaedra tightened her hand around Asta's arm.

"I will be with you."

As they turned to enter the tower they were greeted by a large group of men with angry faces, Gunnar leading them.

"Gunnar!" Phaedra ran to him expecting open, welcoming arms. Instead he took her by the arm and escorted her away.

The other men led Asta into the hall and toward the fire pit where Jorund was sitting at the table. She could see the tension in him before he spoke.

"Is it true?" he asked her without looking at her.

Something was wrong, for he was extremely angry. "Is what true?"

He finally looked at her, but not with the love he had been showing her. Instead it was pure hatred in his eyes. He knew. Somehow he had found out before she had the chance to tell him and now he hated her. She took a step back, not wanting to have this confrontation with everyone looking on. A hand on her shoulder stayed her.

Jorund stood and walked to where she was.

"Please, Jorund, I need to—"

"Is it true?" His voice boomed and echoed through the open tower.

She clasped her hands together and looked him in his eyes. "Yes, it's true. Jarl is my father. But—"

Jorund held up his hand, his eyes dark and cold. "He is your father?"

Her heart stopped. "I thought you knew."

"I only knew you were one of them. The symbol on the daggers I took from you matched the symbol on the ship's sail." His face twitched with the anger that she watched double in his eyes. "Go to my room and stay there until I come for you." He turned and walked away.

"Please, Jorund, just listen to me."

He stopped but didn't turn. "Go now, before I lose control of my temper."

Asta stayed for only seconds before she turned, head held high, and made her way up the stairs with everyone watching.

Asta sat on the bed letting the tears flow free. She knew it would be like this. The people here needed vengeance for the wrong done to them years ago, and she would be the one who was punished. Or would she? If she left, Phaedra would be fine. After all, she had been bought from a slave owner, making her nothing more than a slave herself.

Asta wiped her face clean then retrieved the trousers and shirt she had stashed in the chest. After dressing, she removed the brick from the wall to get the medallion. When she was ready to leave, she stripped the bed of all the fabric, tore it into strips, and then braided it into a tight rope. She tied one end to the heavy bedpost and dropped the other end out the window.

The cold stone at her throat had her thinking twice about running away. But the image of anger in Jorund's eyes overrode that thought. She unclasped the necklace from around her throat and laid it across the bed. One more look around the room, then she climbed out the window and down the side of the wall.

Just past the herbs of the garden was a secret door. The same secret door her mother had snuck them out of so many years ago. It was overgrown with weeds and ivy, so she reached blindly through it, feeling for the latch. Her hand came in contact with it and she twisted it until it gave then pushed the door with all her strength. It moved slowly, grating across the ground as it went.

She stopped and waited to hear the voice of anyone who was nearby. When none came, she squeezed through the small opening. There was no one around, for they were all gathered in the great hall deciding her fate.

She pushed the door back to its locked position. From here she could see the path that led down to the beach where the boats were docked. She made her way slowly to the beach, hiding among the shadows from the few people who where moving toward the tower to see what the commotion was about. The guards had even abandoned their posts and, to her relief, some had left their swords. She took one and continued on to the farthest boat near the pasture. She turned to see the tower one more time. She had been wrong to love him, wrong to think he loved her too. He wouldn't even listen to her, let her explain. Where was Dania? Why did she not tell him? When she did tell him it would be too late, she would be far away. Her only regret was not saying good-bye to Marynn.

"Are you going somewhere, Asta? Or is it Karis now?"

She knew that voice. It slithered down her spine with nauseating fear. She turned to see the only person she ever feared standing a few feet away.

"Torum."

She lifted the sword, but he was too fast. He grabbed her wrists and twisted them behind her back, her sword dropping to the sand. She could feel his breath on her neck as he talked.

"You have been a bad girl, Asta." Torum's hand tightened, pulling her closer to him. "This time Jarl isn't around to hear you scream, so scream all you want."

Asta took a deep breath to do just that, but something was quickly tied around her mouth.

"When we get to the ship, but not now."

Her hands and feet were bound then she was handed up to Torum and thrown across his horse. There was nothing left but despair for her. Torum would surely kill her this time, but first he would torture her.

They rode into the darkness of the forest and she watched as the tower disappeared into the fading light.

Dania was out of breath by the time she reached the gate to the village. The guard at the gate saw her as she motioned him over.

"I…need you to…get my son," she demanded in between breaths.

The guard stared at her as if she was a crazed woman.

"Get him now!" she growled through clenched teeth, ready to lose her temper.

The guard turned and ran through the village to the tower gates. Within moments Jorund was riding toward her. He jumped from his horse, a look of concern on his haggard face.

"Mother, what has happened to you?" He reached for her head, pulling twigs and leaves from her tangled hair.

"I ran all the way here. It's Marynn. I went to see her and there were men at her cottage. They carried weapons and shields."

Jorund mounted his horse and two others, with Gunnar taking up the back, followed him as he made his way out of the village. He stopped and watched as his mother made small steps behind them.

"Where are you going?"

Dania raised her chin, prepared for an argument. "With you. I need to know she is alright. If you don't take me I will walk."

Jorund stared at her a moment then, with a big sigh and a roll of his eyes, he lifted her up onto his horse.

When they arrived at Marynn's all was quiet. The men dismounted, swords drawn, and made their way to the door. It was slightly ajar so Jorund pushed it open all the way with his foot. There was Marynn on the floor surrounded in a pool of blood. Dania ran to her friend, kneeling down to see if she still lived.

"There's a pulse."

"Gunnar, you take care of Marynn, you two come with me." Jorund and the two men searched the surrounding forest for signs of the intruders while Gunnar did his best to stop the bleeding.

Gunnar ripped open Marynn's dress to better see the wound. "She's been stabbed."

"Those men were looking for my Karis."

"Hush now, Marynn. Don't try to talk."

"Dania, you must listen. They remember me. They know she's here."

"What is she talking about?" Jorund entered the room and looked at Dania.

"Where is Asta?" She asked him.

"She's at the tower. What's going on?"

"We need to get her to the tower. I need my supplies." Gunnar lifted Marynn into his arms and carried her out.

"I will ride back to the tower with you and tell you everything I know." Dania followed Jorund to his horse and they headed back to the tower.

"Marynn's real name is Lucia."

"Lucia? As in Olaf and Lucia?"

"Yes, and Asta is really Karis, their lost daughter." Dania felt Jorund tense.

"No, she said herself that Jarl was her father."

"Not her real father. During the raid Jarl followed her and Lucia into the forest. He took Asta, or I should say Karis, and raised her as his own."

"Are you sure? Why would you not tell me?"

"I myself only found that she was alive when you brought her here."

"And Lucia?"

"She wished to be left alone and unknown. I kept to her wishes by being silent about her true identity."

Jorund was silent as memories of a young girl floated to the surface of his mind. Dark hair and blue eyes. "Have I met Asta before?"

"Yes, once when your father and I visited shortly before the massacre."

"I remember her." Guilt once again surfaced in his soul. "I condemned her in front of everyone. I thought she was a spy. She had the daggers on her, daggers that bore the same dragon and sun as the ship that fateful day. Gunnar had seen them again on the sails of the ship in the next village."

"When was this?"

"He returned today at—"

There was a pause before Jorund's grip tightened on Dania. He kicked the horse into a full run leaving the two men with Gunnar and Marynn. They went through the village gates straight to the tower without slowing, people jumping out of the way as they rode.

Once inside Jorund dismounted, lifted his mother down, and then ran into the tower and up the stairs to his room. The door was locked so he called out Asta's name. When there was no answer, he slammed his shoulder into the door, breaking it, and entered the room. The window was open, a makeshift rope hanging through it. A sparkle caught his eye from the fading sun and he looked to the bed. There lay the opal necklace he had given Asta. He picked it up, cursing the bed, and then went back to the hall to ask if anyone had seen her.

Dania was standing at Phaedra's side explaining to her what had happened. He knew by Phaedra's expression that she knew more than she was telling. He made his way across the crowded hall, arriving as Dania was finishing her story.

"So I ran back here as fast as possible. When we went back we found Marynn on the floor bleeding. There was no sign of the men."

"Did you see what they looked like?" Phaedra asked, hoping it wasn't who she thought.

"There was about five or six. The leader was big, with short blond hair."

"Did he have a scar across his cheek?"

"Yes, but how did you know?"

Phaedra began to sway as the buzzing in her head grew louder. Strong arms grasped her and helped her to a bench. Her head started to clear and everything Dania had told her came rushing back. "Where's Asta?" She turned to face Jorund who was sitting on the bench next to her.

"She's gone, left out the window." Jorund never took his eyes off of Phaedra. "If there's something you know, you need to tell me. Is she in danger?"

"She wouldn't be if not for you. She didn't want to tell you because she said you would not listen, none of you," Phaedra yelled to the now packed room. "She wanted to tell you, but she said you would seek vengeance. She was right. You condemned her for something that was not her choice." Phaedra was hysterical now, afraid for her friend.

Jorund shook her until she had some control over herself.

"I need to know if she is in danger. Please, Phaedra, I love her."

With that admission, Phaedra did not hesitate to tell Jorund the truth. "Yes, she is in much danger. His name is Torum. He's Jarl's nephew." She looked at Dania with sorrow on her face. "He's also Jarod's son, the boy you were to meet that day you came to the tower."

The color drained from Dania's face. "Are you sure?"

"Yes. His mother's name was Sorna. The night we left, Asta went to Jarl's tent. He told what he could before he passed into the next life."

"That means he's..." Dania looked to Jorund.

"My brother."

"If he finds her he will kill her."

Jorund immediately went into action, separating his men into groups to search the land.

"I wish to help." Bruno stepped forward, concern etching his face. "My brother and I have travelled all this land and know many people."

"That would be much appreciated."

Gunnar was still tending to Marynn, so Dania and Phaedra took it upon themselves to volunteer to search at the beach. They walked past the arena to the ships, but Dania's hand on Phaedra's arm stopped her.

"How much do we need to worry, Phaedra?"

Phaedra didn't want to be the one to tell Asta's story or her punishments, but her silence had caused too much trouble as it was. She took a deep breath to tell the story that had been weighing on her soul.

"It was Jarl that sent you that note. Sorna died in childbirth and Jarl spent every day letting Torum know who was at fault."

"Jarod."

"Yes, and that is why they came. To Jarl, everyone here was at fault for accepting what he saw as disgrace to him, his sister carrying the child of his enemy. When she died, it made him a little crazy in his head. He was set on revenge no matter the cost. So they set sail. What he didn't count on was finding Karis. She reminded him so much of his own daughter that he had lost just that year. He decided to take her home to his wife, Eriel. She was so pleased that they raised the child as their own, changing her name to Asta. Torum took this as a sort of betrayal by his uncle. He would torment Asta everyday. Than, one winter, Erial became sick. On her deathbed she made Jarl promise to protect Asta and teach her to fight as he taught his warriors. He agreed and that sent Torum into a rage. He started punishing Asta with embarrassing comments at first, but soon it got out of control. He would physically harm her when they were alone, which was often. She had become a great warrior and Jarl decided to leave it to his nephew to watch over her."

"Jarl didn't know what was happening?"

"No, and Asta wouldn't tell him. She was afraid it would make Torum worse. He would tell her that if she didn't do what he asked, he would punish me instead. I was bought by Asta as a slave and that was all anyone ever saw me as. As much as I begged to take her place she wouldn't have it, so when she returned from his torture we, me and the other slaves, would take care of her."

"If she was such a good warrior, then why didn't she fight him?"

"She was and is the best I have ever seen, better than even Jarl. But there was one better than her. Torum. They were both trained by Jarl, both shown the same techniques, but Torum was just a little better."

"The scars, that was his punishment, wasn't it? He cut her, didn't he?"

"Yes, but that wasn't the worse thing. Torum wanted to marry Asta, to have total control over her. Jarl wouldn't have it and started to become suspicious. It wasn't long after that he fell ill. With Jarl too weak to lead, it fell to Torum. He went behind Jarl's back and announced that he would marry Asta. We escaped that night with another of our friends, and over a dozen of Torum's slave girls. It was bad enough we took them, but for Asta to leave would be a slap to his face. How was he to explain to all of his men that Asta, the girl that they admired, ran off to avoid marrying him?"

"Now he is here to take her back?"

"Yes."

"Not without a fight." Jorund came up behind them, a torch burning bright in his hand. "Do you know where she would go?"

"I think she may have taken one of the ships."

They went to the beach, Jorund checking to see if any boats were missing. "They're all here."

Dania kicked the sand and her toe met with something hard. She reached down to retrieve the object. "A sword?"

"Look!" Phaedra pointed to the hoof prints that led through the pasture. "It looks to be four or more riders."

They followed the path until it led into the forest.

"They're headed to the next village. That's where Gunnar saw the ship. Come on." Jorund ran back to the tower, the girl's right behind them. None said a word about Asta. They already knew Torum had found her.

Asta lay face down on the ship, her hands and feet aching from the tight rope that held them. Her back was stinging and she could feel the blood as it dripped down her sides. It became dark not long after she was taken, giving Torum the opportunity to start her punishment without prying eyes. As she rode across his horse he had ripped open her shirt, baring her back. Each cut with the knife was to remind her that he controlled her and she could never escape.

Now she watched him as he paced back and forth beside her.

"You have been a lot of trouble, Asta. It has taken my time and money to come for you and you will pay it back." He leaned down and brushed her hair from her face. "In whatever form I decide."

It was getting dark again and they had been out to sea for hours. With each minute that passed her hope of being rescued dwindled. She closed her eyes and pictured Jorund. She should have told him that she loved him. Now she would never have the chance. But instead of dwelling on that, she concentrated on the image of his bright smile.

"You look almost happy, Asta. If you are thinking that Jarl will help when we arrive, you are wrong. He is dead. Passed away the night you left. Don't worry; you will be taken care of." Torum's evil laugh scared her more than anything.

She knew of Jarls death of course, but with him gone there was no telling what Torum was going to do. She closed her eyes and took a deep breath. She would not give him the pleasure of seeing her in pain.

Ian rode as fast as he could back to the village. He had to tell Jorund what he had seen. The sun was barely rising so it took a moment for the guards to answer his impatient pounding on the gate.

"Hold, boy. Do you see it's still early?"

The gates slowly opened and Ian ran at full force toward the tower, tripping once but catching himself before falling. Dania was the first person he saw upon entering the hall.

"What's your hurry, Ian?"

His arms swung wildly as he tried to explain his emergency to Dania.

"Slow down, I don't understand."

"What's wrong with him?" Phaedra was making her way down the stairs. She approached Ian with great concern.

"I don't know. I can't understand him. He came running in out of breath and agitated about something."

"You have to calm yourself, Ian." Phaedra tried to stir him toward the cookery but he wouldn't have it.

There was no time for their guessing games so, with a deep intake of breath, he let out the only word he had spoken in years.

"Asta!"

Both women stared at him, stunned. From his sudden outburst of sound or the name, he wasn't sure, but the message was loud and clear. It was Phaedra who spoke first.

"You've seen Asta?" Phaedra held his shoulders to keep him still.

He nodded his head yes and pointed out to the water.

"They took her out on a ship?"

Ian nodded his head again in confirmation.

"Did you see which way they sailed?"

His head moved again, but this time in aggravation.

"I have to go after her," Phaedra said to Dania. "I can't wait for Jorund."

"He may have found her already."

"No. He was going to the village. If Ian says they were sailing then Jorund had to have gotten to the village too late. Torum is not daft. He knows someone will come after her, even if that someone is me. He would not take the chance of losing her again."

Ian began swinging his arms again and pulling Phaedra toward the door.

"I will be heading out as soon as possible."

"I will get our supplies."

Phaedra looked back to Dania.

"You didn't think you were going alone, did you? And I think Ian will have to come along too since he can point us in the right direction."

Again Ian confirmed this with a smile and a nod of his head.

It was late into the night when Jorund, followed by Gunnar and his men, rode wearily into the village. The search for Asta had not gone well.

After riding through the night, they came upon the seaside town where Gunnar had seen the ship, only to find the ship had set sail that morning. To make things worse, nobody had seen a girl fitting the description of Asta.

As they entered the gates to the tower and dismounted, the young kitchen girl Reah came running across the yard.

"My laird!" She came to a stop a few feet from him. "I told them not to go. I told them they should wait but they wouldn't listen."

"What are you babbling about?" Jorund's anger was to the boiling point and his body too tired to deal with any more problems.

"It's Phaedra and Dania."

"What about them?" Gunnar quickly came to Jorund's side when Phaedra's name was mentioned.

"Ian came early as the sun was rising. He had followed the men who took Asta. He led Phaedra and Dania in their direction."

"What?"

"Where?"

"They rode out to the east."

The men remounted their horses, and with a renewed burst of energy, they were on their way again.

They arrived a few days later in a small town of the eastern coast. Phaedra dismounted, motioning for Ian and Dania to do the same. She took two large hats from her saddle bag, put one on and handed the other to Dania. They had dressed as men, donning large cloaks and trousers for safer travel.

"It will be sunrise in a few hours so we must hurry." Phaedra secured her sword to her side and waited as Dania placed her daggers in their hidden encasements. She knew the ship was here, for she could see the sails from where she stood.

"Ian, you take the horses back through the forest and hide until we return. If you are spotted then ride. Go back to the village and tell Jorund where we are. Do you understand?"

He nodded his head and moved the horses back through the darkness.

Phaedra started through the village with Dania following behind. Moments later they were close enough to the beach to see the entire ship, its sails glowing in the moonlight.

"What now?"

"The ship looks abandoned. If I know Torum, which I do well enough, he is out celebrating his victory over Asta."

"How do you know he is not aboard?"

"If he was they would be sailing. The question is how long do we have before he returns? There are two guards that I can see, both at the bow of the ship, and no other men aboard. The others will be in the town. Listen."

Both women leaned against the building wall listening intently to the laughter of the inebriated drift to them.

"We don't have much time. When the sun rises they will make their way back to the ship." Phaedra started forward. "Follow me and do what I do."

Phaedra spotted an abandoned bottle next to the building and picked it up. As they neared the ship she began to wobble using the bottle for show. Dania quickly imitated Phaedra; both looking like two drunkards who could fall at any minute. They began to board the ship and, to Phaedra's relief, the men had also been drinking. They drunkenly made their way to block the entrance to the ship.

"Who goes there?" one of the men asked in slurred speech.

Phaedra stepped forward.

"Captain said to retrieve the girl." She wobbled to her left, hoisting the bottle up as if she were drinking, then threw it to the ground to make them think she had just finished. The other man stepped forward, tripping over his own feet.

"He said nothing to us."

"I can go back and tell him you said no, but the next time we dock, you will be in this same position."

"What position?" the first man asked curiously.

"Sitting here, watching the ship without a woman to warm your body."

The two men looked to each other, shook their heads, and then went back to their makeshift tables to drink again.

Phaedra and Dania looked around the ship but saw no signs of Asta. They lit a small lantern and made their way below deck to the hold. It only took minutes for them to find her there. She was behind a large curtain at the back of the ship, on her knees with her feet and hands bound. She wore only a white chemise that was covered in red stains.

"Asta?" Phaedra knelt down next to her friend.

At the sound of a voice, Asta's head slowly came up. The gasps that came from Phaedra and Dania were loud in the stillness of the damp room. Bruises marred Asta's face and neck and trailed below her tattered shirt.

"Phaedra? Are you really here?" Asta's voice was barely audible.

"Yes, I'm here. I told you, you can't leave me."

Asta looked past Phaedra to Dania who was trying to hide her shock and dismay. Panic rose in Asta's expression.

"You must leave. He will kill you both."

"Everything's going to be alright." Phaedra turned to Dania. "The knife. We need to cut the ropes."

Dania hurried over to Asta and, kneeling beside her, began to cut at the ropes. Phaedra stood looking around for something to cover Asta. She settled with the curtain and tore it from its hooks. She wrapped it around Asta and helped her to her feet.

"Lean on Dania, she can take your weight. I'm going to lead us out of here."

They made their way above, Phaedra taking on her drunken manner once again. But the men were too far into their spirits to notice them leaving. The three of them worked there way through the town under the shadows of the buildings and through the trees where Ian waited for them. He helped Asta mount his horse then joined her, helping to hold her up as they rode away.

The sun rose and then set. Still they rode, not wanting to stop for fear of who may be following. It was hours into nightfall when Phaedra turned her horse deeper into the forest.

"Where are we going?" Dania motioned for Ian to follow Phaedra then fell in behind them.

"When we first came here, we stayed in an old abandoned inn. It's hidden well by overgrowth." Phaedra looked back to Ian and Asta. "We need to rest before they fall from exhaustion."

It seemed they rode for a long time before the old inn came into view. There it stood, large and imposing in the dark night. Phaedra dismounted and approached Ian's horse.

"Let me help you down, Asta. Ian, do you think you can care for the horses? There's a creek behind here. They will need water."

He nodded his weary head and dismounted. Phaedra and Dania helped Asta inside while Ian gathered the horses and led them around the back to the decrepit stables.

Once inside the inn, Phaedra led Asta and Dania through the dark to the back room that held some wood from their last visit. Dania put her cloak on top of a pile of leaves then she helped Asta lay down on her side while Phaedra stacked the wood in the hearth and started a fire.

"No one should be able to see us this far in, even with the fire burning. The night will hide the smoke."

Ian returned from the stables with an old bucket full of water and pointed to Asta.

"Thank you, Ian."

Phaedra took the bucket and set it next to Asta. She and Dania knelt beside Asta and, armed with their knives, began to cut away the blood-stained chemise.

"What has he done to you?" Dania's eyes filled with tears as she looked at Asta's bare back. Every inch was black and blue with over a dozen deep cuts scattered over the soft flesh.

"Please, Dania, don't cry. I'm safe now." Asta's voice was just a whisper.

"We are not safe until we are back at the tower." Phaedra ripped the stained chemise into pieces then took the cleanest part and dipped it into the water to clean Asta's back. An hour later she was done. Dania began bandaging Asta's back with pieces from her cloak.

"He has the medallion, Phaedra."

"We don't need to worry about that right now." Phaedra pulled the curtain up to cover Asta. "You just rest."

Phaedra motioned Dania away from Asta's side.

"We need to keep watch tonight. We will leave when the sun first peeks over the horizon. I'll keep first watch, you second, and Ian can take third."

They both looked to where Ian was curled at the foot of Asta's small bed fast asleep.

"What was she saying about a medallion?"

"When she was taken by Jarl, her mother had given her a gold medallion. She managed to keep it hidden all these years from prying eyes. It is a map of your land stones, only we couldn't figure out where it leads to."

"I know of this medallion."

"How?"

"I have the piece it fits to."

Phaedra was stunned by this confession. "How did you come by the missing piece?"

"I told you I was friends with her mother. She entrusted it to me, thought it was safer if the pieces were separated."

"Did she tell you what it led to?"

"She spent many years looking for the end of the map but never found it. I think I should tell you, Marynn is Asta's mother, Lucia."

"What? Are you sure? Why wouldn't Marynn tell her?"

"I have known since the day of the attack. I was the one who found Lucia and helped her to regain her health. She wanted no one to know so we changed her name and she moved to the old cottage."

"Does she know Asta's her daughter?"

"Yes, but she felt she needed to gain Asta's trust before telling her."

"Asta should know. Marynn needs to tell her when we return."

"If she can, though Gunnar did say she should pull through."

"For both their sakes I hope she does. Now go rest. I will wake you when it is your turn to watch."

It was almost sunrise when Ian came running into the back room waking Phaedra and Dania. He had heard horses coming their way and now the three could hear the angry mumble of men's voices as they approached the building. They rose from their makeshift beds. Dania positioned herself in front of Asta's sleeping form, her sword drawn, ready to defend. Phaedra stood by the door, her sword raised, prepared to strike, while Ian put himself at the back of the room ready to charge whoever dared enter.

They stood in the dark listening to the approaching feet. The door burst open and for a moment there was silence.

"I need some light, I can't see anything. Bring me a torch."

"Gunnar, is that you?" Phaedra lowered her sword as the torch cast light on the room and the intruders.

Gunnar entered followed by half a dozen armed men. Phaedra dropped her sword and threw her arms around Gunnar. He embraced her with his strong arms then set her back with a stern look on his face.

"You are to never leave like that again. I will not permit it."

"But Gunnar—"

"Quiet. I will not hear of it."

Dania stepped forward, eyeing each man. "Where is Jorund?"

"We separated to search for you. He took the other half of the men with him."

"Ian?" Angus entered the room and Ian flung himself into his father's embrace. "Son, what are you doing here?"

"Asta." The word was spoken softly, but it didn't take away from the surprise everyone was feeling at hearing the young boy speak. "Asta," he said again, this time pointing to the still form lying on the floor.

All turned as Dania moved for them to see.

"By Thor, you did it. You found her." Gunnar walked closer with the torch and almost cried out in horror at the sight before him. The woman lying there was almost unrecognizable. Every inch of her skin from head to what he could see of her was covered in dark blotches. Many pieces of cloth had been placed on her back and were spotted with blood. "What happened to her?"

"Torum and his twisted mind." Phaedra stepped forward and looked upon her friend with much love.

"I would like to know how you came to take her back, but that is best saved for later. We need to get back to the safety of the tower. How do we transport her?"

"She has been worse, though you can't tell by the looks of it. She will ride." Phaedra knelt next to Asta. "It is time to leave now, Asta."

"I know. I have heard everything. I wanted to lie here as long as possible," she said, beginning to rise.

Phaedra removed her cloak and gently put it around Asta. Then Dania wrapped the curtain around Asta's shoulders and helped her outside.

"I will ride with her." Phaedra mounted her horse and gave Gunnar a look that squashed any argument he had. He said nothing as he helped Asta up in front of Phaedra.

"Lean on me, Asta."

Then, surrounded by the men, they made their way back to the tower.

Days passed, then a week, and still no word came from Jorund. Asta's wounds began to heal, her bruises fading from black to grey and yellow, but her heart still ached with the need to be in Jorund's arms. Everything that had happened since her departure was explained to her, including Marynn being her mother. She passed the days talking with Marynn, who was still recovering from her almost mortal wound.

"Why did you not tell me who you were if you knew who I was?"

"I wasn't sure of the life you had led or if you would even accept my word to who I was. You were so young when they took you."

"They did this to you?" Asta ran her fingers over Marynn's scarred face.

"Yes."

"I hate them for what they have done to all of us."

"I have had a good life regardless. My only pain is that I didn't have you and your father."

"Tell me about him."

"Your father, Olaf, was the son of a highborn of Dal-riata. His mother was a lowborn, worth nothing unless on her back. When she became pregnant, she was sent away to the land of the Picts. It was there she found a man who loved her and her unborn child, your father. Together they made a family. Your father was taught to fight and defend. When he was older, war broke out among the land. He was asked to take care of the only living descendant of the rulers of Pictavia."

"You?"

"Yes, I was the grand-daughter of a great king. This was his land. Once we were wed, your father became ruler here. He was a just ruler and the people loved him. That's why it is so hard for them to let go of their need for vengeance."

"I remember him, but only vaguely."

"He loved you with all of his heart. He had a picture of the sacred standing stones permanently colored onto your skin to be sure you would always remember where you were descended from."

"What of the medallion? Do you know where it leads to?"

"That is something the women in my family have been trying for centuries to discover. I once had an old journal that I would study and write in, but it is long gone, burned in the fires of the raid."

"I remember the journal. I remember the night you took me to the stones with you. I rubbed my hand across the circle etchings in the stones."

"That was to be the first of many nights. I wanted you to continue the search for whatever it was the medallion was made to hide."

"I have been searching, but only as far as you have made it. I don't have the piece anymore. Torum took it from me."

"That is fine. It is in my memory. I know exactly what it looked like. When things are back to normal we will have plenty of time to study our findings together."

"Will it ever be normal again? The festival has stopped and yet the people stay."

"Jorund is a good ruler. He brought peace to this and the surrounding lands. They will not leave until he is safely back here where he belongs. If that means they spend the winter here then that is exactly what will happen."

"You think he will be gone that long?" Asta's heart dropped at the thought of so much time passing before she could see him.

"No, he will return soon. Gunnar has sent men to find him and tell him of your return. When he hears this he will race back swiftly."

Asta would leave Marynn throughout the day for she was still weak and in much need of rest. At these times while Marynn slept, Asta would practice her sword with Phaedra. Gunnar didn't mind as long as they did this in the courtyard where they were safely behind the wall. The men were still in awe of the two women's experience with the steel, but they would no longer stop and gawk when the two practiced.

It was on a clear warm day as they did their usual swordplay that they heard commotion coming from the village. The tower guards had opened the gate and the girls watched as the guards, along with the villagers, ran to the front gates.

"What's happening?"

"I don't know, but I'm going to find out."

Phaedra followed Asta through the village, dodging panicked people as they ran.

"They act as if we are under attack."

"We are."

Phaedra looked over to see Gunnar approaching them, a look of pure hatred on his face.

"Who is it?" But Asta was sure she knew the answer to that question.

Gunnar looked at Asta, not wanting to tell her, but he knew he had no choice. "Torum and he has Jorund."

Asta felt as if the ground had disappeared from under her, but somehow she found herself running to the gates and climbing the ladder to the watch station. Sure enough, there was Torum and about a hundred of his men. Between them, tied to the side of a wagon, was a beaten and bloody Jorund.

"No!" The sound of her voice echoed down to the men and Torum turned around, smiling coldly at her stricken face.

"Asta, or is it Karis now?"

"What have you done, Torum?"

"I have done nothing. This is your fault. If you had not escaped I would not have come for you and found your mate on my way." Torum raised his hand and brought it down hard on Jorund's already bloody face.

"Stop, please."

"If you open the gates to permit us, I will not hurt him or the others."

Asta hadn't noticed the group of prisoners the men had under their swords. All the visitors who had been set up outside the walls for the festival were now herded like sheep to one side.

"It's happening again. He's going to slaughter them all just like he did before." Asta turned to see Gunnar's stricken face as he looked out to the men, women, and children.

"No, I will not let it." She turned back to Torum. "If we open the gates you will kill them anyway and everyone inside."

"Perhaps. Do you have another suggestion?"

"Yes. I will fight you for their freedom."

"No!" Jorund's voice boomed out above all other noise.

"You would fight me? And if I win, what do I get?"

"Me. I will come willingly with you."

Torum's cackling laugh echoed through the air. "It's a deal. Come then, meet with your fate."

"Not quite yet. Your men must let the people go. They are to enter the village as I exit. If any of your men try to enter with them, the guards will shoot their arrows to kill."

"And if you do not come out, I will slice your beloved friend's throat while everyone watches." Torum emphasized this by placing his sword to Jorund's throat.

"Agreed."

Torum thought on this a moment before answering with a wave of his hand. "Let them go."

Asta climbed down the ladder and met Phaedra at the bottom.

"Do you remember how he fights? You were the only one as good as him, Asta. I know you can bring him down."

"You can't be serious. He will kill you. There has to be another way." Gunnar put a hand to Asta's shoulder but she shrugged it off.

"You would do the same."

Asta took her sword from Phaedra and waited for the guards to open the gate. When the people came through she made her way out, warily watching Torum's men for any of them to attack her. But none did. They knew her, had grown up with her. She could see the doubt in their eyes, but as much as they respected her, their fear for Torum was more. She made her way to the middle of the clearing where Torum waited.

"Do you really think you have a chance?"

"Both you and I know that no one can take me when I have a weapon."

"I think I have proven I can."

"Only when you are sneaking up behind me like a coward."

"You little—"

"You made a mistake."

"How's that?" he growled, coming closer.

"You let me live."

He slowly pointed his sword toward her. "So what happens now?"

She raised her sword to him. "One of us will die."

He was the first to strike, hard and heavy. She knew how weak she still was, for her arms quivered with the force, but she would not stop. She raised her sword and struck back.

Her instincts and expertise from years of fighting quickly came back and she let herself become the warrior she was trained to be. As the fighting escalated, so did her hatred for this human who called himself a man. She watched carefully for any mistake he might make.

Torum's sword came down on hers with another bone-shaking blow. She knew she had to do something quickly. He was trying to tire her out, she knew, for that was always his way of winning. He struck again, harder than before, or maybe it felt harder because the baby was draining her energy.

The baby.

The thought hit her harder than any blow he could give. She had only realized today herself and was still in shock. But that thought gave her an extra boost of energy. She waited for Torum to strike again. When he did, she side-stepped his move and brought her sword down hard on his shoulder. The sharp blade sliced through his skin, opening a deep wound.

Asta stepped back, stunned by the agonizing scream coming from him. Never had she heard this sound come from this wicked man. The fear she had once felt for him slowly faded to nothing. She circled Torum as he reached for his sword with his other hand. She swiped her sword across his other arm, causing him to drop his sword and fall to his knees.

"How does it feel, Torum, to be on the receiving side of pain? Are you enjoying this?"

His skin was pale, his face a look of pure hatred mixed with extreme pain. His wounds were bleeding immensely and his arm hung limp where she had struck him in his now gaping shoulder. She pushed his sword away then knelt down in front of him.

"I want you to be the first to know. I carry his child."

"No! When I recover I will be back to kill him and the child."

"That is something you will never do." Asta lifted her sword and brought it down hard across Torum's neck, severing his head from his body.

EPILOGUE

Jorund paced back and forth in the hall waiting for Dania to come and give them word.

"You must calm yourself. Women go through this all the time and she is stronger than any I have ever met, besides my Phaedra." Gunnar glanced toward his wife where she sat on the bench rubbing her protruding belly.

"Thank you, my dear husband, but I am sure you will be in the same mood when my labors begin."

The wailing of a baby above brought all in the hall to their feet. Moments later Dania descended the stairs.

"Jorund, would you like to meet your son?"

"A son?" Jorund moved up the stairs with the speed of the wind. He entered his room to see his beautiful wife sitting up in the bed, a small bundle in her arms.

"Come, meet your boy." Asta motioned for Jorund to sit next to her on the bed, then she handed the baby to him.

"I have a son." He smiled widely as he looked down into the baby's sleeping face. "What shall we call him?"

"I was thinking of Jarod, after your father."

"Jarod my baby boy."

"Then, when we have another, I thought we could name him Olaf."

"What if we have a girl?"

"We will have to keep trying until we have another boy."

Jorund leaned down and kissed his wife. Never had he been so happy in his life.

"I have something for you." He handed the baby back to Asta and retrieved a box from under the bed. He opened the box to show her.

Inside was the medallion, both pieces locked together.

"You have given me the greatest gift and I wanted to give you something in return."

"How did you find it?"

"One of Torum's men gave it to me the day they left. He said he knew it meant a lot to you."

Asta reached for her husband and kissed him with all the love in her body. She knew now that she was truly home.

Made in the USA
Columbia, SC
12 November 2025

73224445R00104